To Our Readers:

We have been delighted with your enthusiastic response to Candlelight Ecstasy Romances®, and we thank you for the interest you have shown in this exciting series.

In the upcoming months we will continue to present the distinctive sensuous love stories you have come to expect only from Ecstasy. We look forward to bringing you many more books from your favorite authors and also the very finest work from new authors of contemporary romantic fiction.

As always, we are striving to present the unique, absorbing love stories that you enjoy most—books that are more than ordinary romance.

Your suggestions and comments are always welcome. Please write to us at the address below.

Sincerely,

The Editors
Candlelight Romances
1 Dag Hammarskjold Plaza
New York, New York 10017

A Candlelight Ecstasy Romance ®

"WHY'D YOU COME?"

Evasively, she lowered her gaze. "I was restless . . . out walking . . . I saw your light . . ." She groped for a feasible excuse.

"No, Blair," Matt murmured, his fingers gliding within her hair. "You were out walking . . . remembering . . . and suddenly you felt compelled to be with me."

Her skin tingled with his touch. "Please, Matt, don't do this. I'm weary of the game. I don't want to hurt or be hurt anymore."

With an easy move he pulled her close against him. "I think our fears are mutual." His hands began to explore her back in a meandering caress. "We both know why you came; you wished it and I willed it." His body melted nearer. "Dear God! How I've wanted you," he confessed, his voice husky, nearly grieving. "This moment may hurt us both, but for all the empty ones, can't we chance it?"

A CANDLELIGHT ECSTASY ROMANCE ®

MEMORY AND DESIRE

Eileen Bryan

A CANDLELIGHT ECSTASY ROMANCE ®

Published by
Dell Publishing Co., Inc.
1 Dag Hammarskjold Plaza
New York, New York 10017

Dell ® TM 681510, Dell Publishing Co., Inc.

Candlelight Ecstasy Romance®, 1,203,540, is a registered
trademark of Dell Publishing Co., Inc.,
New York, New York.

ISBN: 0-440-15608-4

Printed in the United States of America
First printing—November 1983

To a classic and exemplary example of a strong and sensitive woman—my friend, my peer—Sharon Lloyd

CHAPTER ONE

There is that secret part of everyone's life that would be better forgotten—haunting, hurtful memories that we tuck away in the recesses of our minds and never revisit. Blair Hayden was no exception. She had spent the past ten years of her life trying to escape the taint of Farrett's Corner. Yet, oddly enough Blair was now racing her Ferrari over secluded back roads, headlong into the very past she wished to deny.

For the most part she'd been successful in erasing the small-town stigma that branded her as wild and socially unacceptable riffraff from the Hollow. For in the tolerant world that existed beyond the clannish hill country, Blair was known as Jess Hayden's widow—heir to the oil baron's millions and a power to be revered.

She had never aspired to such a position. In fact, she hadn't ever dared to dream of wealth. Her underprivileged youth had taught her that such dreams were reserved for those who had a chance of making them come true, and the daughter of an Ozark tenant farmer certainly had no chance at all.

"Blair Lee," her papa would say, "seems like some of us were born to scrimp 'n' scrape, 'n' others to gather the harvest. Ain't our place to be questionin' why. I reckon it's decided upon by someone bigger than us. Sooner you set your mind to rest and quit frettin' over what you can't

change, the sooner that gnawin' inside of you will cease."
Her dead father's words droned in her head much like the
hum of the sports car's precision motor. It had been ten
years since she'd traveled this dirt road, yet the winding
trail was as familiar as the earthy smell of red clay. It
seemed that neither time nor miles could outdistance certain memories.

Such abstract thoughts filled Blair Hayden's mind as
she wove her way across the shell parking lot and braked
to a halt at the bottom of the hill ascending to the Pavilion.
Pale moonlight slivered through a thicket of poplar trees
and giant pines to cast an opalescent sheen over the silent
countryside. Only an occasional shrill of crickets and the
faint sound of music drifting down from the Pavilion
broke the stillness. The clear summer night carried the
fresh scent of flowering dogwood, and the mountain air
felt cleansing as Blair breathed deeply.

There had always been a singular quality about the
Ozarks to Blair—almost melancholy. Regardless of the
distance she traveled or the years she'd spent away, it
remained with her. Its purple, gold, and mauve landscape
colored her dreams and lured her restless nature. To out-
siders it was the Shepherd of the Hills country, but it was
home to the unassuming Blair Logan of the Hollow, and
it would be a test of inner strength for the sophisticated
Blair Hayden of Dallas.

Blair's gold-flecked gaze lifted upward to the Hilltop
Pavilion. Instinctively a warning chill ran the length of her
spine. She knew that just as the beauty of the hill country
had remained unchanged, so had the mores of Farrett's
Corner. The small-town people with their small-town
minds would never change.

12

A soft night breeze stirred, carrying the lone cry of a whippoorwill. It swayed the gay Japanese lanterns decorating the Pavilion and rustled the welcoming banner that was stretched above the entrance. Blair's solemn eyes lingered on the inscription. FARRETT'S CORNER WELCOMES THE CLASS OF '70! She wondered if the greeting also included her. Somehow she doubted it. She hadn't had the distinction of being voted most popular or most likely to succeed. But, if there had been a category for most gossiped about or ostracized, she would have won easily. Just the thought of those painful days when she'd been subjected to the vicious whispers, the taunting snickers caused Blair's chin to set in the same stubborn fashion it had in her youth. Even now she tried to pretend that it didn't matter.

She flipped the car door open, and her shapely legs stretched for solid ground, then supported her slender frame as she rose to her feet. The slam of the door preceded her quick inspection of the daring silk original she wore. Quite intentionally Blair had abandoned her usual conservative style and dressed to give her classmates something to gawk at. After all, they'd always considered her borderline scandalous. Why should she disappoint them now? Golden glints became dominant in her hazel eyes. Jess had often remarked that the characteristic reminded him of a lioness—proud, yet leery. His description was never more accurate than tonight. At a thoughtful gait Blair proceeded up the hill.

Marybeth Simmons interrupted her nonstop tirade on the evils of the new liquor-by-the-drink ordinance recently passed by city council, just long enough to raise her second gin-and-tonic to her motor mouth. Then, suddenly, her jaw went slack and her enormous eyes bulged in disbelief. The glass hung suspended inches short of her lips as an unrecognizable sound that resembled something between a croak and a hiss escaped her.

"I don't believe my eyes!"

Instantly everyone at the table turned to gape at the stunning redhead poised in the doorway.

"As I live and breathe . . . Blair Logan. I'd recognize her anywhere." Rachel Davis, now Mrs. Lloyd Prentiss of Prentiss Hardware, identified the object of their stares.

"Ain't such a mighty job recognizin' her. 'Pears to me she ain't aged a day, let alone ten years." A man of few words and little tact, Rachel's normally subdued husband ventured a dry comment.

"Hmmph!" Rachel scoffed. "That's just the kind of remark I'd expect from you, Lloyd Prentiss. As I recall, there was talk of you chasin' that red-headed nymph in your wilder days!"

"Way I heard it, Lloyd had lots of company." Mason Hershell, who was only tolerated in the tight circle of friends because he'd happened to marry Lurlene Desmond, the preacher's daughter, spoke up. A nervous laugh went up from the men. The women shot each other knowing looks.

"Ain't no secret, Mason. Blair Logan had a reputation around these parts. Some say she wasn't as bad as has been made out; some say she was worse. Only thing I know for sure is"—Arley Simmons gave his wife a reproachful look —"there's been a lot said."

She promptly ignored his remark. "I for one am thinkin' her reputation was well-earned. Never heard her deny it, did you? Course not, cause she can't. She was always flauntin' herself around school, puttin' on airs like she was somethin', and all of us knowin' she came from that trash down in the Hollow. The boys trailed her like hounds on a scent. Only because they knew she was easy and willin'."

"Know that for a fact, do you, Marybeth?" Arley's voice took on an edge that escaped his wife.

"Well, tell you what I know," interjected the meek Lurlene Hershell. "I know that rumor has it that both the Farrett brothers were involved with her, and to this day Matt Farrett blames her for Luke's death."

"For a fact!" Rachel Prentiss confirmed, leaning forward in her chair as if to share a choice tidbit. The women instantly became alert, scooting their chairs closer; the men feigned indifference but kept their ears cocked.

"Lucy Michaels has been doin' some private nursin' out at the Farrett place. Seems old Miz Farrett's been gettin' worse and is pret' near bedridden now. Well, anyways, old Miz Farrett confided in Lucy that Matt still harbors a terrible bitterness about Luke's death. Says even though Luke met his end in Vietnam, he really died here in Farrett's Corner. 'N' what's more, said that he died of a broken heart and the prideful miseries 'cause Blair Logan made him the laughingstock of Taney County!" Rachel sat back in chair, a "tsk tsk" look on her face.

"The Farretts ain't to be taken lightly under the best of circumstances. To have Matthew Farrett for an enemy would be courtin' trouble." Arley looked over at the redhead under discussion, who was still standing alone and stately by the door. A look of empathy swept his plain features. "Seems like a hard accusation, but I don't guess

Matthew Farrett's the kind of man who'd blame without good cause."

"Course not," Marybeth snapped back at her husband. "'N' you mark my words, her comin' back here's gonna cause trouble for all of us. Farrett Mines support half this community, and the last thing we need is a riled-up Matthew Farrett to contend with. Can't believe she'd have nerve enough to show her face in this town again. Especially at our ten-year reunion, when she knows darn well that Matt will be attendin'. I think the woman's taken leave of her senses."

Rachel Prentiss's eyes followed Blair as she moved toward the refreshment table. "Well, I hope she's not bankin' on a warm reception. It'll be a cold day in—"

"I doubt she's countin' on it," her no-nonsense husband broke in. Scuffling to his feet, he excused himself with "I think I'll check out the refreshments. Don't imagine it'd hurt anythin' if I just tell Blair hello."

"Lloyd Prentiss, you sit yourself right back down here!" the flustered Rachel sputtered. "Lloyd, you hear me! . . . Lloyd?" The others at the table traded uncomfortable looks. Each of them knew that Lloyd's insubordination would be the topic of a heated debate in the Prentiss household later that night.

Sauntering up to the spiked punch bowl, Lloyd cast a testing smile in Blair's direction and then eased into idle conversation. "Looks as if time's been kind to you, Blair Logan." He held up the dipper suggestively, his smile broadening as she nodded in acquiescence. Clumsily he passed her a cupful of the fruity concoction.

"Thank you, Lloyd. I might say the same of you."

"You might, but we'd both know you'd be stretchin' the

16

truth." He grinned boyishly, reminding Blair of the carefree Lloyd Prentiss she'd known eons ago. They sipped their punch tentatively, aware of the many pair of eyes upon them. Lloyd's face remained impassive, but his voice held a warning note when next he spoke.

"Your surprise appearance at this affair has set folks back on their heels a little, Blair. You've rattled the whole passel of 'em by showin' up out the blue like this."

"I can only imagine." She smiled, a benign smile that did not quite reach her almond eyes. Lloyd couldn't help but be momentarily captivated by her remarkable beauty. She'd always been attractive, but now she'd matured, come into her own as a woman. The end result was overwhelming for a prosaic shopkeeper. He gulped another mouthful of punch, then ventured a glance at his wife's forbidding profile.

"How is Rachel?" Blair intuitively inquired.

"Pushin' thirty and ten pounds heavier," he replied with his usual candor. "Guess most of us have changed—some for the better, some not." He hesitated, as if weighing something that lay heavy on his mind. "Blair . . . I . . ." He faltered, but then rallied when he met her quizzical gaze. "There's something I've often wished I could say to you but never thought I'd get the chance."

Intrigued, Blair set aside her punch cup and gave him her undivided attention. He noticed the air of confidence she projected—an acquired quality that she hadn't possessed in her youth. It unsettled him slightly, but he squared his shoulders and continued.

"Guess we all did some mighty foolish things in our youth. I pride myself on havin' grown up some since then. Lookin' back on it all, I ain't too proud of some of my

17

antics. 'Specially braggin' on my womanizin', which was more fiction than fact. Course, I suspect I'm not the only fella guilty of stretchin' the truth so that he could boast of his conquests all over town. It was wrong, awful wrong, buildin' our egos at your expense. You could've set the record straight and shown us all up for the fools that we were, but you never did. If it's any consolation to you, there are those of us who regret our malicious lies." He met her astonished look with sincerity.

"You're right about one thing, Lloyd—we all did some foolish things back then—me included. I wanted attention so badly that I settled for the only kind I could get—notoriety. Besides, no one would have believed me even if I had tried to defend myself."

"Probably not. Folks around here do most of their judgin' minus the facts. Why did you come back, Blair?" His bluntness took her off guard. She'd been away too long and had forgotten the straightforwardness of the hill people. Again, she smiled, her pouty lips seeming to smother a secret.

"For many reasons, Lloyd. Like you say—some good, some not." Lloyd was about to delve further into the mystery when the new Methodist minister walked up to them.

"Evenin', Reverend Akins," Lloyd greeted him, stealthily slipping his doctored punch behind his back and easing it onto the table.

"Mr. Prentiss." The pastor astutely averted his gaze, allowing Lloyd an opportunity to discard the incriminating evidence. Tall herself, Blair had to look up into the animated face of the young preacher. There was an innate strength that emanated from the healthy tanned face that

18

was smiling warmly back at her. His manner hinted at subtle humor, yet his clear, indigo eyes shone with a perceptiveness that was quite unnerving. All this she noted in a matter of seconds.

"Could it be possible that Farrett's Corner has adopted another newcomer beside myself? I hope so, I've been in the minority for far too long." His hand stretched out to her, a large, reassuring hand. She took his hand, without really understanding why she felt so naturally inclined to do so.

"Heck no, reverend. Why, Blair here grew up with all of us. She lit out of town right after graduation, is all."

"I'm disappointed. I'd hoped to find a comrade in Blair. But perhaps we might still find a some common ground and discover that she's a Methodist?" He winked mischievously at her, producing an amused glow upon her china-doll complexion.

"Blair Logan! A Methodist! She's from the Hollow. Ain't nobody from Hollow ever been anythin' other than Baptist. It goes against the grain. You won't be makin' a convert out of her." Considered half-heathen himself, Lloyd loved to play the devil's advocate.

"Blair Logan the Baptist, is it?" the reverend drawled in a refined Southern voice.

"Blair Hayden," she corrected him, glancing at the astonished Prentiss.

"When'd you get hitched, Blair?" Lloyd asked with customary directness.

"Shortly after I left Farrett's Corner," she replied.

"Hayden," the reverend repeated thoughtfully. "You wouldn't be any relation to the Texas Haydens of Hayden Petroleum, would you?"

"Yes . . . Jess Hayden was my husband," she answered, surprised that he had made the connection. "Are you acquainted with the Hayden family?" Blair made a point of ignoring Lloyd's gaping mouth.

"No, not personally. They were members of my father's congregation for a time in Dallas. I was sorry to hear of Jess Hayden's death. From every account I've heard, he sounded like a truly fine man."

"In every sense of the word." A distant look crept into Blair's sensitive eyes. Unlike Lloyd, the reverend did not miss it.

"I hope you're not from one of those strict Baptist sects that denounces dancing?" The young reverend assertively removed his black jacket and stood before her in his shirt-sleeves.

Suddenly Blair became aware of the music filling the room, but no more than she was acutely alert to the disapproving eyes that bore down on them. In her mind, two inner voices vied for attention: the reserved Dallas socialite argued caution, but the former rebel from the Hollow urged her to accept. The old rash tendencies won out, and it was the impetuous Blair Lee Logan who smiled demurely when accepting.

"Since we're to be partners, can I call you by your first name, Reverend?"

"My parishioners call me Rev Akins; my friends, just plain Jim." He cocked a brow toward the dance floor, where a few couples swayed awkwardly.

"I'll reserve judgment until after we've had our dance, Rev Akins. Stomped toes have deterred more than one budding friendship." With a challenging toss of her copper hair, Blair led them center stage as Lloyd wandered back to the nest of vipers.

"I'd say that the only one making a bigger fool of hisself than you tonight, Lloyd Prentiss, is Rev Akins!" Rachel glared at her disobedient husband across the table as he returned to his chair.

Lurlene Hershell visibly paled. "You're bein' a mite unfair to the reverend, Rachel. Bein' a newcomer to Farrett's Corner, how's he to know that Blair Logan's a hussy? Just look at her—bewitchin' him with those cateyes and clingin' like he was her salvation. Poor Rev Akins!" Since her own father was a man of the cloth, Lurlene felt obliged to speak up in the reverend's defense.

"I tell you, she ain't changed a bit. She's still chasin' anythin' in pants—even to a man of God. Blair Logan's shameless!" Marybeth huffed indignantly.

"She ain't Blair Logan," Lloyd Prentiss corrected smoothly.

"Have you been samplin' that punch a tad too much?" Lloyd smiled to himself at Marybeth's hypocritical censure of his drinking habits. Everyone knew that she habitually got tipsy.

"No, Marybeth. Just merely statin' the facts. Blair goes by the name of Hayden now. Got married a while back." He leaned back in his chair, enjoying the group's reaction —stunned silence.

Always a calculating individual, it was Mason Hershell who remained collected enough to worm the pertinent facts out of Lloyd. "Hayden, you say. I once read about a Texas oil clan by the name of Hayden. Couldn't be the same family though. They're society folks." His black eyes narrowed appraisingly.

21

Lloyd tilted the chair back on its hind legs and glanced out onto the dance floor, where Blair and Rev Akins were two-stepping. His response was slow in coming and seemingly directed at no one in particular. "I don't why you'd think that was so farfetched. Weren't y'all just spoutin' off on how connivin' Blair can be? What makes you think a rich man's any less susceptible to"—he paused dramatically, shooting each of them a reproving look before adding, "to her *kind* of woman?"

"Oh, for Pete's sake, Lloyd," his wife clucked. "Is she hitched up with those oil Haydens or not?"

"She was—" he began, his remark igniting an audible murmur around the table. But before Lloyd could explain further, the pious Lurlene Hershell cut in.

"A divorcee . . ." she supplied in an appalled voice. All eyes traveled to the couple who were leaving the dance floor—the harlot and her unsuspecting prey. "Poor Rev Akins!" Lurlene lamented.

"There you go, jumpin' to conclusions, Lurlene," Prentiss scolded, impatience shading his voice. "A widow—she's a widow," he clarified.

"Well, that don't surprise me much," Marybeth stated smugly. "It appears she has a real talent for puttin' a man in an early grave—just like Luke Farrett. Misery just naturally follows that one, I tell you." She fortified herself with a sip of her third gin-and-tonic—a cure to ward off the evils of Blair Hayden.

"Oh, shut up, Marybeth! Next thing you know, you'll be spookin' everyone with your superstitions." Over the past five years Arley had learned to read the early-warning signs of his wife's intoxication. From past experience he knew it was time to muzzle her.

22

Mason Hershell was shrewder than the others. His position as vice-president at Farrett Mercantile Trust caused him to be much more interested in Blair's connection with the Hayden wealth than her lethal effects on men. Perked with curiosity, he sat straighter in his chair and eyed the scandalous redhead with a little more respect.

Aware of the adverse attention they were drawing, Blair subtly tried to discourage the reverend's lingering attentiveness. "I think your parishioners are feeling neglected, Reverend. Perhaps, you should mingle some."

Jim Akins possessed an intuitiveness that went far beyond his theological training. He was aware when the inflections in a person's voice contradicted her words, and he noted the reflections of the soul in a person's eyes. Consequently he was neither fooled nor surprised by Blair's supposedly casual remark.

"You've been away far too long, Blair," he laughed. "Few of my flock are here this evening, and they're not among those you worry yourself with."

Again Blair found herself drawn to this solid man, not understanding why, not even questioning the phenomenon. She was about to explain her concern when some magnetic force drew her eyes to the doorway and the shadowed silhouette of the man who'd just entered. Her pulse quickened, and her breath grew scant. Before he'd even stepped from the night shadows into full view, she knew it was Matt Farrett. She knew by his commanding stature and the agility with which he moved. But, more than this, she was warned by the feeling of helplessness that overcame her. There was only one man who could induce this effect—only one, and, God forgive her, he was the one and only man she'd ever truly loved.

23

Jim Akins noticed the tremble of her hand upon the punch cup before she raised her other hand to steady it. He also noticed the yearning expression that lit up her green and gold eyes. He had seen that kind of longing before—regret mingled with despair.

Matthew Farrett strode into the Pavilion as if he owned it. For, in fact, he did. His masterful presence seemed to fill the room all at once. Heads turned, conversations lulled and then slowly resumed in whispers as acknowledging smiles were flashed in his direction. He paid no heed to the atmosphere of respect he inspired. Such things were second nature to a man like Matthew Farrett. Beneath the sun-streaked hair that feathered his brow, his crystal-blue eyes shone cool and aloof. They were the eyes of a realist, seconded by a strong, uncompromising profile. Standing tall, broad-shouldered, and lean, he looked every inch a living legend. And so the Farretts were—a legend that spoke of class distinction and power.

The only other person in the room who could match Matthew's affluence, as well as his fierce pride and strong will, was Blair. The clash of these two opposite yet equal forces seemed predestined. So when from across the room Matthew's ice-blue eyes locked with the defiant gold in Blair's, it was inevitable that the very air between them became electric. Matt's jaw grew taut, his whole person snapping rigid with both shock and anger. Blair's chin rose, her mouth set to still its quivering and meet the challenge in Matthew's unwavering gaze.

Reverend Akins looked from one to the other. Being attuned, he sensed the tension immediately. His own heart beat a little quicker as he watched Farrett's purposeful approach. He looked to Blair, whose expression remained composed and determined. He'd been acquainted with Matthew Farrett for some time now and had never known him to be unjust or violent, but, suddenly and irrationally, he felt afraid for Blair Hayden. His grave eyes darted about the room, observing the glazed excitement with which the vigilant townspeople watched on. They appeared to be awaiting some kind of showdown. It sickened and panicked him. But before the reverend could react, Matt's hand clamped around Blair's upper arm possessively, and he curtly excused them with "You'll pardon us a moment, Reverend."

Momentarily disconcerted, Rev Akins stammered, "I, ah, well, that is . . ."

"We won't be a minute" came the brusque reply as Matt all but dragged Blair away. A worried sigh escaped the pastor as he noted the rebellious tug Blair gave to wrench free of Matthew's hold. The undeterred manner in which Farrett led her outside the Pavilion doors and beyond his protection did little to alleviate his concern. Yet, though he knew his apprehension to be justified, some wiser voice told him that this confrontation was meant to be. Grudgingly he resisted his compassionate impulse and did nothing to alter the course of events.

Once sheltered from the prying eyes inside, Blair jerked clear of Matthew's grip. She stood willful and unintimidated before him. Though her cheeks were stained with embarrassment, she managed to retain a note of complacency in her voice.

"If I'da known how anxious you were to renew old acquaintances, Matt, I'da called on you first thing." She rubbed her smarting upper arm with a smirk. The only indication of the anxiety she felt was the ease with which she slipped back into the Hill dialect. She often did so when uncertain of her ground. Not having been exposed to the cosmopolitan Blair, this revealing lapse went unnoticed by Matt. Much like the unseen hurt that she carried deep within.

He scanned her from head to toe, his eyes unkind and his entire manner demeaning. "The only thing I'm anxious for is the sight of your back as you leave Farrett's Corner. I gave you credit for better sense than to tread on Farrett territory again. Now I'll give you some invaluable advice—get, and get quick, while you still have the chance. I may not be so charitable tomorrow."

"I'm not frightened by you, Matthew Farrett!" she challenged. "I have every right to be here. It's as much my town as yours."

The tendons in his neck constricted as he ground out, "Not anymore, Blair. You forfeited that right ten years ago when you never looked back to see the harm you caused. Now get out of my sight before I make you regret that I ever laid eyes on you!" The moonlight only served to illuminate the cold rage that marked his angular features. Before her loomed a man of granite, hard and unyielding. The unmistakable intent in his eyes caused her to cringe inwardly, but outwardly she pretended indifference.

"I'm going nowhere but home, Matt Farrett. So, when you come with the tar and feathers to run me out of town, you'll know exactly where to find me. Hope you enjoy the reunion as much as I did. Night." With a flip of emerald silk and auburn hair, she marched past him, her unsteady legs barely accomplishing their purpose as she descended the hill.

Matthew remained rooted on the Pavilion porch. Several indecisive seconds passed while he stood ramrod straight and stared out across the widening gap between him and a ten-year-old tormenting memory. Then a low curse accompanied the frustrated slam of his fist against the wooden pillar. At last he turned and went back into the Pavilion.

"Told you!" Rachel Prentiss hooted, pointedly nodding toward the doorway in acknowledgment of the fact that Farrett had just returned alone. "I knew he'd send Blair Logan packin' in short order."

"It's Blair Hayden," Lloyd corrected, his voice as lifeless as his expression.

Marybeth slammed her fourth gin-and-tonic to the table with a woozy splash. "Her name's mud, thas what, Lloyd Prentiss. And if you've a lick of sense, you'll steerrr clearrr of her, less you've a mind to tangle with Matt Farrett!"

"Don't you reckon it's time for us to be departin' this shindig, honey?" Knowing his wife's capacity as well as her tendency to become belligerent when drunk, Arley tactfully tried to stage-manage a timely exit.

"I ain't ready, Arley," she whined. "Besides, I haven't even bid the reverend . . . hell—" She hiccuped, weaved in her chair, then balanced her elbows on the table and added an anticlimactic "—o." The others tried to act as if they hadn't noticed, more for Arley's sake than for hers. Hardly anyone paid any attention when Festus Crawford pulled up a chair and joined them.

"Howdy! You folks enjoyin' yourselves?" he greeted them, swapping a huge chaw of tobacco from one cheek to the other.

"Yeah, it's been a fascinating gathering of the clan." Mason Hershell couldn't resist an outsider's innuendo.

Not very intelligent and even less astute, Festus plunged ahead. "Guess y'all know'd Blair Logan's back in town. Pulled into my station early this mornin' in a fancy rig. 'Fill 'er up,' she says, without so much as a howdy or how've you been."

"Yeah, we know. She was here in the flesh," Mason curtly cut him off. Local morons bored him.

"Well, betcha you don't know who she brought with her? Mighty interestin' too." Festus's brown-stained teeth seemed to fill his whole face.

"Who?" To everyone's surprise, it was Lurlene Hershell who begged for the tantalizing details.

"A fella," Festus crooned, coyly waiting to be coaxed.

"Well, is that all you're gonna say?" Rachel's curiosity caused her high-pitched voice to sound frenzied. "It's a cinch he ain't nobody from around here. What'd this fella look and act like?"

"Well, let me recollect." Festus lured their attention as he appeared to ponder the questions. "As I recall, he was a small fella. Can't tell y'all much about how he acted, cause he was snoozin'. But I can tell you for sure what he looked like. Or better yet, *who* he favored." He hesitated, drawing out his tale to gain the fullest impact.

"Damn you, Festus Crawford! Quit stallin' and get on with it!" Marybeth eloquently expressed the entire group's sentiments.

"Okay, okay, I'm gettin' to it. You ain't got no cause to get so testy, Marybeth." Festus pretended to drop his wily tactics. "She had a boy with her, and judgin' from his red hair, I'd say he was hers all right."

"Blair Logan? A child?" The barren Lurlene practically wailed the words.

"Yup! And there's more." Festus had everyone's attention now and was reveling in the seldom received recognition. "I got three younguns of my own—all boys. So, I figure I'm qualified to be speculatin' on this whelp's age. If I were a bettin' man . . ." He glanced surreptitiously into their skeptical faces, then hastily affirmed, "Course I ain't. But if I were, I'd stake all I own that the boy was right at ten—not quite, but comin' up on it. Food for thought, ain't it?" Again he grinned, but this time not a soul at the table noticed his grimy teeth.

"Don't suppose any of you, ah, righteous gentlemen feel a Christian urge to own up?" This time Festus Crawford laughed aloud, a mocking cackle that pierced the suddenly stifling air. To the upstanding alumni of Farrett's High, the only thing more repugnant than the sight of the vulgar Festus Crawford was the grating ring of his solitary laughter.

CHAPTER TWO

The pale pink of breaking dawn mated with the low-hanging mist hovering in the valleys, their early-morning marriage veiling the surrounding hillsides in shadows of cool lavender. The warble of a red-breasted robin as he issued his own mating call echoed through the dewy-leafed trees. While, in the distance, the lonesome bay of an old hound rang out. The Ozark summer morning had all the appearances of normality, all except for the forlorn figure of a man who was standing on his balcony and hypnotically gazing out upon the day's birth. This daybreak, Matt Farrett didn't experience the rejuvenating effects of an Ozark dawn. In fact, he didn't see it.

As he looked out across the spectacular landscape he only saw the ghostly images that had driven him from his restless bed—the faces of an unforgettably beautiful woman and a grotesque, no longer identifiable man. The visions haunted him. So much so that there seemed to be no escape, no place that offered respite. Matt rested a foot on the terrace railing, an arm on his knee, his head in his hand. He was so weary of the memories, so tired of wrestling a ten-year bout with his conscience. *If only Blair hadn't returned.* For now he was torn between two conflicting emotions: He either loved Blair or hated her. He was no longer sure which.

His sleep-starved eyes lifted in the direction of the Hollow—the lair of the beast that stalked him. He remembered the gangly, mop-haired tomboy perched high up in a tree and giggling as he toppled from his horse beneath her. He'd sprang to his feet, silencing her with a bullying glare while dusting off the seat of his trousers. Then she had smiled, a sunshine smile that left him warm all over. Rhythmically swinging her unlaced tennis sneakers, she'd merely said, "Some mighty fine ridin', Matt Farrett. You just need to learn an easier hand with a filly." The memory of the incident caused that same warmth to rush over Matt once again. He winced and looked away from the Hollow.

Rubbing his aching temples, he eased himself upright. The golden dawn had broken fully now, its radiance crowning the peaks of the mountains and lighting up the cloudless sky. It would be many hours before its brilliance twined through the densely wooded valleys. By then he would have put in a full day at the office and, presumably, taken care of the other matter that haunted him. With a shrug of his shoulders he turned from the grace of the hills and strode through the terrace doors back into his bedroom. He looked upon the disheveled covers—a crumpled testimonial to his state of mind. Unwillingly his gaze moved to the picture frame that rested atop his dresser—a photo of his brother, Luke, the last one ever taken. An emptiness consumed him.

Luke smiled back at him from the gilded frame, a dashing figure in his military dress greens, yet a far cry from the pacifist he'd aspired to be. *And what had caused such a change in a man?* "Blair Logan" the bitter whisper came as reflexively as the unspoken question. Matt walked to the dresser and took the picture in his large hands. Numbly he sat on the edge of the bed, staring and thinking.

The sensitivity still shone in Luke's blue-green eyes, but the lighthearted smile no longer curved his lips. That had disappeared with Blair Logan's departure from Farrett's Corner. Luke had loved her. He hadn't been ashamed to admit it. He'd befriended and defended her, unlike Matt, who'd taken her, and then, in a moment of confusion, deserted her. *At least Luke was spared the knowledge of his own brother's complicity.* He'd never known of Matt's previous involvement with her. *No, thank God, Luke hadn't realized that, in his own peculiar way, his younger, more callous brother loved her too—just as Blair herself had never known.* It was probably the only good that ever came of the disastrous triangle. For had Luke known, it would have devastated him; had Blair, she would have been elated. She could so easily have made fools of both Farrett brothers, instead of just one.

As it was, Luke never got over Blair's desertion. He forsook his heritage and enlisted in the Army. Matt doubted that Luke had anticipated being sent to Vietnam, but once his orders came through, he seemed to complacently accept his fate. Acceptance always grew easier after disappointment.

Luke never returned from Nam—except as another statistic in the form of an official notification from the Department of the Army, a few personal effects forwarded by his commanding officer, and a heart-wrenching memorial service held by the local V.F.W. chapter. There was nothing left of him to send home—no part of Luke Farrett to even return to consecrated ground. The pieces that once made up the whole of a man were scattered over some rice paddy in an unknown part of the world.

The photo in Matt's hands blurred before him. He

32

couldn't help but wonder what Luke's last thoughts had been. Did he think of home, so different from his oriental place of exile? Or at the instant of his death did he visualize the lovely face that he'd sacrificed himself to? For as surely as if her hand had stretched across the miles, it was the touch of Blair Logan that had sent him to his death. The black-shirted Viet Cong merely accommodated her by planting the land mine. In actuality, it was *Blair, Blair herself* who had delivered him up for execution. Renewed bitterness surged through Matt as he rose to his feet and replaced the picture frame atop the dresser.

How many men's souls would it take to satisfy Blair Logan? he silently cried out. The mute admission shook him to the core. Defeatedly he slumped back upon the feather mattress, burying his head in his hands. Though he and his brother shared the same fate, each had suffered differently at Blair's hands. Luke's resolution came swiftly and thoroughly. While he, Matt, was damned to a living purgatory where no solace could be found.

In her youth Blair had possessed a kind of naive sensuality which caused the very best and worst in a man to surface. Now, matured and more beguiling than ever, the passionate magnetism she conveyed was even more potent. She represented the most dangerous of adversaries, one who held the greatest advantage of all—a still strong influence on Matt's heart.

Anguish turned to resolution within his azure eyes. Hauling himself to his feet, he bolstered a slim reserve of inner strength with a solemn pledge: before the sun set on this day, he'd settle the score with Blair Logan once and for all!

* * *

33

Depending upon which vantage point one viewed an Ozark sunset from, the effect could vary tremendously. From the Hollow, which lay nestled and almost somnolent in the valley, its burnished splendor accentuated the majesty of the hills. Elongated shadows from the densely timbered knolls slowly wound across the countryside, shading neatly plowed fields and weathered barns. Gazing out over this tranquility from her perch on Gram Logan's porch railing, Blair was once more poignantly reminded of her own insignificance. She sighed and futilely tried to clear her troubled mind.

This earthy place was home, a stabilizing force that at this time in life Blair needed. For along with the sorrow that lay ever present in the shadows of her mind, there were mingled many fond memories. The land itself, the sweet rolling green of the hills and the brown, furrowed turf of the valley, this was good. The robust caress of the Ozark breeze as it ruffled wisps of her flame hair and eased beneath her open shirt collar to fan her bare breasts, this was natural. Then there was Grams, the best thing of all about the hills. She'd yearned so long for the sight of her paternal grandmother's lined and sun-bronzed face.

Blair stretched lazily, her eyes trailing into the distance toward the secret blackberry patch where Grams and Danny strolled. A smile stole across her full lips—a tender smile that she reserved for those whom she dearly loved, like Danny and Grams. She had no doubt that by now Grams was weaving some of her magic folklore, the same tales told to her as a child. Her smile broadened as she imagined Danny's delight at hearing the nostalgic yarns. He was so much like her. Blair knew that in the years to come Danny would recall and treasure these easy summer

34

days shared with his great-grandmother. The old matriarch's hill spirit would pass on to yet another generation, and her simple strength would sustain him.

She propped a foot up on the railing, folded her arms around her bent knee, and leaned back against the rough cedar upright. Danny! How she loved that child. It was almost sinful to love a son in such an exclusive and consuming way. It left little room in her heart for anything or *anyone* else. Jess had understood, but then, wise and loving, Jess had understood everything about her so well. God! She missed him terribly, his companionship, his strength. She'd grown to love him in a quiet, comfortable way. Often she wished she'd told him, even though she knew in her heart that the words would have been unnecessary. For he'd realized long ago that she cared, and her affection seemed to please and nourish him to the very last. But she couldn't help wondering what he'd think of her recent behavior. Would it have surprised him? No! He might have been concerned, but never surprised.

The evening whistle blew at the mines, its solitary shrill resounding from hill to hill and down into the valley. The wailing sound knifed through Blair in much the same way the memory of Matt Farrett often did late at night when she lay alone and tossing on her widow's bed. She had successfully banished those recollections from her marital bed, stubbornly denying Matt any space between her and Jess. Not that Jess hadn't known of Matt's existence or of her past, neither of which she could or would have denied. From the very beginning, and all through their relationship, honesty prevailed. It was upon this sacred trust and mutual respect that she and Jess had built their union, admirably triumphing where others failed.

Reflexively Blair's gaze rose to the distant hilltop on which Farrett House stood. A wistfulness highlighted the green in her eyes. Impulsively she stood up, the single thick braid that cascaded down her back swinging with the abrupt movement. Wrapping an arm about a cedar post, she reflected upon a time when things stood differently between her and Matt Farrett—a brief, but unforgettable period in their lives when barriers lifted, lovers came together, and consequences were ignored. It was natural and good, like the scented breeze of the Ozark evening that stirred her sensitive skin, like the steadfastness of the rich earth beneath her feet. But then, reality had closed in and youthful hesitancy dictated the future. The end result had been calamitous for them both.

The faint ring of a cowbell as Grams's old Jersey made her way to the barn recalled Blair from the past. She had learned long ago that it did little good to think on what once was or might have been. For it always brought back the pain of what had actually happened and what would never be. The handsome youth she had idolized so much that one spring became the vindictive man who over the years had nurtured an unjust hatred and sought to have his revenge, the very same man she came to Farrett's Corner to deal with and, secretly, prayed to be exonerated by. Maybe then, and only then, could she lay to rest the confused feelings that continued to plague her. The postponed confrontation would happen. He would come. This she knew as surely as every dreading heartbeat. The time was near. She could sense it.

A stir of dust rising a short way up the lane, along with an instinctive tightening in the pit of her stomach, gave Blair her answer. She came fully alert, her heart pounding

36

and adrenaline racing. Wiping her damp palms across her Wranglers, she watched in masochistic fascination as the Cherokee bore down on her. It seemed as if she were peering into her own destiny—a destiny rushing toward her on the surety of four-wheel drive.

With a final squeal of brakes and a creak of the jeep door, the tall figure of Matthew Farrett broke the road haze. It took all the self-control Blair possessed to casually lean one shoulder against the post and hold her voice steady as she forced a cool "Evenin', Matt. I've been expecting you."

Without the slightest hesitation he paced off the distance to the covered porch and stopped short of the steps, legs astraddle and glaring at her. "Glad you're prepared, Blair. It'll save us a gang of energy and a lot of small talk."

"Small talk never was your style. Care for a glass of lemonade? Been a touch warm today." The screen door swung open, and she disappeared from view.

Infuriated at her refusal to be cowed by his bullying tactics, he cleared the steps two at a time and then banged the screen door with menacing whack. "We can skip the refreshments right along with the weather report." Matt's angry frustration mounted when he noticed Blair's inattentiveness as she continued to pour the token drinks. "Last night I warned you to get out of Farrett's Corner, today I'm telling you!"

"This ought to be to your likin', Matt—sour to match your disposition." She held out the glass of lemonade, an impudent grin on her ripe lips.

Before she could blink, his hand came up, knocking away her offering and sending it crashing to the kitchen floor. "This is all some kind of game to you, isn't it?" he snarled, his sharply defined features transmitting total disgust. "Some sick, perverted sport to amuse the retired town tramp!"

Blair's eyes snapped, but the pseudo-smile remained fixed upon her sultry mouth as she bent to pick up the shattered pieces of glass.

"What's the matter, Blair? Did you run out of space and men to use? Or is it that the easy hillbilly gal didn't score too well in the big city?" Stooped before him as she was, her head lowered, her silence only served to enrage him more. His steel grip encircled her wrist, hauling her upright with a wrenching jerk. "Answer me, damn you! Why did you come back?"

A piece of jagged glass still clenched in her hand cut deeply into her flesh, but stunned by the way he was manhandling her, she was too preoccupied to notice the warm trickle of blood running down her arm. Matt's frigid gaze moved from her stricken face to the red streak that dribbled from her fingertips. "Damn you!" he cursed, pulling her over to the sink without relaxing his grip. In one swift motion he whipped on the cold water with his free hand and doused her lacerated fingers beneath the spray until the porcelain was tinted pink. In her dazed condition she continued to clutch the broken glass as if it were a life preserver.

"For Christ's sake, Blair, drop it!" he ordered, and immediately the shard of glass fell with a tinkle to the sink.

They avoided each other's eyes while standing shoulder to shoulder. Matt continued to grasp her wrist, in a tourniquet fashion, as Blair stared dumbfoundedly at the unreal mingling of her blood with the cool liquid. At last the sound of the water faded, and Matt's sure hands wrapped a cup towel about her wound.

"I think some antiseptic and gauze will do," his voice droned through the vacuum that filled her head. "Now," he said, regaining some of his composure. "I don't really care why you've come. I want to hear you say that you're leaving."

Her detached gaze locked with his, her voice sounding oddly detached as she murmured, "I did have a reason for coming back here. I came to offer you a business proposition."

Matt's face lost all trace of expression, and his soothing touch was withdrawn as he stood impassive and expectant.

"It's barite that brings me to Farrett's Corner," she announced, slowly regaining her poise. "You have it, and I need it. It's that simple, Matt."

"What in the hell are you talking about?" He slumped back against the counter as if he'd been dealt a blow.

His question was a valid one. *What in the hell was she babbling about?* she wondered. But once she had brought the subject up, she elected to follow through. "I thought by now you'd have heard of my connection with Hayden Petroleum?"

He smirked. "Oh, I heard all right. So, what has your new status got to do with barite?" Matt insisted on making her appeal as difficult as possible.

"The petroleum boom has created a critical shortage in virtually all associated materials—supply cannot keep up with the demand. I'm sure I don't have to explain how crucial barite is to drilling, nor how few and far between the sources are." She tried not to sound patronizing. She could tell by his perplexed gaze that she was handling this all wrong. *Damn!* The whole scene was ludicrous. "I'm searching for a supplier of barite." The tactless admission burst from her lips of its own volition. Quickly she rushed to amend her urgent tone. "An arrangement between us could work, Matt. I'm prepared to offer you—" His incredulous laughter cut off the rest of her proposal.

"Barite! You came back to negotiate a barite arrangement between us?" Now his laughter bordered on the sinister. "Lady, you're either the most egotistical conniver that ever lived or the biggest fool to draw breath. Whichever, you're a loser, sweetheart! I wouldn't supply you with the time of day!"

Blair's chin rose—egotistical, maybe; a fool, in some ways; but a loser, never! The defiant gold in her hazel eyes virtually glowed as, for the first time, she retaliated. "I wouldn't be too hasty, Matthew. A time may come when you might find a joint venture with Hayden Oil advantageous."

"Joint venture, is it? My, but you have moved up in the world—fast games for high stakes. I think I'd rather deal with a rattler. But if I ever find myself in the position of having my back to the wall and my only alternative financial suicide, I might consider the offer. Don't hold out any hope, Blair. The possibility's remote." His expression grew cynical, his jaw more pronounced.

"That stubborn pride has cost you in the past, Matt. Maybe you should take the time to hear me out." The capable and persuasive businesswoman persisted, even though the girl from the Ozark hills felt an overwhelming sense of defeat. A crimson stain began to seep through the cup towel. Her hand throbbed, and her head ached. *Give up!* her pride screamed, but all the while her valiant heart cried, *Hang in there! Fight!*

"You've got the answer you came for. Now there's no reason for you to stay any longer. I expect to see you gone from Farrett's Corner as quick as you can pack up." He studied her for a brief moment, not with interest, but appraisingly, as if he wondered if she would submit so easily. Then with a contemptuous look he turned and walked toward the screen door.

"I'll leave Farrett's Corner when I'm damn good and ready, Matthew Farrett—not a minute sooner or a second later!" she cried defiantly, tossing her head back and holding her slim form erect.

Without turning to face her, he stopped short of the door. Feeling certain that it was only her incorrigible sassiness which had provoked his hesitation, she braced herself for what would follow.

He remained stationary, his rigid back to her and staring out into the yard. A child's laughter drifted through the mesh screen, and instantly Blair felt a cold clutch of panic. Danny! Matt was studying Danny! Tentatively she approached, her mind frantically searching for a diversion.

Slowly Matt turned her in direction, his blue eyes emotionless and riveting. "Your boy, obviously," he sneered before glancing back out at the vivacious, red-haired Danny who was preoccupied with rinsing blackberries under the outside spigot. Blair's breath left her. Helplessly she stood waiting to be hurt like a hunted animal, paralyzed with fear. Finally . . . painfully it came. "Course, I don't suppose you have the faintest idea who his father is?"

His crude remark pushed her over the brink. In two steps she found herself standing in front of him, and with her good hand she soundly slapped the side of his face. The only evidence of her rashness was the rock of his head, and the red imprint left on his cheek.

He tensed, a flash of fire thawing his icy gaze for an instant. Then, almost absentmindedly, he disengaged himself from her and peered back out at Danny. He stood silent for a few interminable seconds before apologizing in a strained voice.

"That was unfair to the boy. Somehow you always manage to bring out the worst in me, Blair."

"I think it's mutual. We do it to each other." Blair wasn't feeling especially forgiving at the moment. Rather she was experiencing sheer terror. She had to distract Matt's attention, stop him from scrutinizing Danny too closely.

But he wasn't responding. His gaze was intent upon her son. He watched as the boy followed Grams's instructions and scooped up a handful of berries, then dunked it liberally beneath the springwater. Suddenly it dawned on him what fascination the boy held for him—the infectious smile, the cut of his firm jaw, the familiar mannerisms. It was as if he had glimpsed his own heredity—the Farrett bloodline—Pop's surviving physical traits and Luke's good-natured smile.

Blair began to shake visibly. She could feel the stark realization that washed over him. When Matt spun on her, she did not retreat. For when it came to her son, she'd take on Matt Farrett as readily as anyone else who threatened his security.

"I'd forgotten how callous you were. But you've made

42

one fatal mistake, Blair—you underestimated how ruthless I can be." The calmness with which he spoke transfixed her. She tried to respond, but fear's hesitation cost her dearly.

"Did you honestly believe that I wouldn't see the resemblance? Or did you think yourself smug enough to breeze into town, strike some kind of a deal with Farrett's Mines, and then skip out of the county before the village idiot realized what'd hit him? Your confidence amazes me, but then, you have an excellent track record when it comes to deceiving men!"

"You're wrong," she blurted out, stepping closer to him in unconscious appeal.

"*I'm* wrong! You're telling me that I've mistaken your intentions? Hardly! Any more than I don't recognize a Farrett when I see one. I suppose next you're going to deny that he's my brother's son—my nephew!"

"Yes, yes, you're mistaken about everything!" She shook her head in denial, her gold-flecked eyes glazed and pleading.

As Matt pushed the screen door slightly open, she clutched his arm and whispered, "Please, Matt, listen to me."

Expressively his hand plucked off her clutching fingers. "No you listen while I explain. Do you remember your Bible, Blair—the passage about an eye for an eye? Well, I'm giving you the gospel according to this Matthew—a Farrett for a Farrett, my brother for your son. If it takes every dime and the last ounce of grit I've got, I'll fight you for custody of that boy. Not because I owe you the heartache, but because I *want* him. He's a Farrett!"

She reached for him once more, but this time she met

43

only the slam of the door in her distraught face. Mortified, she watched as Matt crossed the yard and then paused beside the boy. Danny looked up into the stranger's eyes, a curious smile on his shining face. Blair felt a tug at her heart. Matt's bronzed hand ruffled the boy's curls. For a breathtaking moment he embraced the past and future with a touch. Then, with unaccustomed warmth, he smiled in return, proceeded to the Cherokee, and peeled out up the lane.

Grams's keen brown eyes rested on her great-grandson's bent head and then lifted in concern toward the disappearing jeep. "Daniel, I believe those berries ere about half-drowned. Gather our pickin's and let's be about storin' 'em." She spoke loud enough for her voice to carry beyond the screen door. Blair ran the back of her hand over her blurred eyes, drew a composing breath, and then hurried on unsteady legs to dispose of the shattered glass.

"Hey, Mom, look at all the berries Grams and I picked!" Danny's elated voice followed the slam of the screen door. His dusty sneakers stopped beside her, awaiting her appraisal of his harvest and a commending smile. "What happened? You break something?" He asked the obvious in the taxing way children often do.

She forced a weak smile before glancing up at her son. "Can you believe it? I'm as big a butterfingers as you." For an instant he searched her eyes, as if he saw something unfamiliar to him, but then just as quickly he dismissed his youthful intuition.

"Look at this haul!" Proudly he held up his bucket. "Grams sure knows how to track berry patches. If she'd have been born just a little sooner, I bet she could've been some great Indian scout."

"Now hold on a minute, boy. Just how ancient do you think I be?" From beneath snowy eyebrows Grams's dark eyes fairly twinkled with amusement. "Set your bucket up there on the sink and let your mama clean up her mess whilst you scrub on yourself. You're more purple than them hills out yonder."

With a happy peck on Blair's cheek and a clatter of the bucket into the sink, Danny bolted from the kitchen in blind obedience. Blair retrieved the last piece of glass and walked silently to the trash, shoulders slumped and head hung low to avoid Grams's perceptive gaze. With a tidy swish of her handy mop, the spry old woman finished the task in silence. Then, with a communicative grunt, she set aside the mop and patted Blair's shoulder.

"Come outside and sit with me for a spell," she commanded, in a tone of voice Blair remembered only too well. Like Danny, she obeyed docilely, settling on the steps and listening to the rhythmic creak of Grams's rocker. For several pregnant minutes it was the only sound that passed between the two women.

"I'd be obliged if you'd tell Matthew Farrett that he owes this old woman a glass and the courtesy of cleaning up his messes," Grams stated, never ceasing her constant rocking. Blair did not acknowledge this, instead kept staring up at the dusky sky and brooding.

"Course, 'pears to me that whenever you two meet up there's always some kind of mess left behind." The damp evening air grew clinging, settling heavily all around Blair.

"You know what's between us, don't you, Grams?" Still Blair did not face her grandmother, the sorrow and shame in her voice laying as heavy as the still air.

The creaking of the rocker continued. "I know'd way

45

before the two of you ever did. I know'd when you asked me to unplait your hair for the Sunday social, when you sat for hours perched up in that old oak just to catch a glimpse of him, when you cried yourself to sleep and moaned out his name. I may not be as book-educated as some, but I understand nature—human and otherwise. Yes, honey, I know'd Matt Farrett marked you long before Danny was conceived."

A lump filled Blair's throat, making her next words barely a whisper. "He thinks the child is Luke's." Despairing hazel eyes turned upon the old woman. The rocker's motion momentarily halted, then started again.

"In this old world there's all kinds of blindness, honey. Just like the hill fog hides the paths and makes one lose his way, Matt's own guilt dims the truth from him. That child ain't no dreamer like Luke; he's a survivor, same as Matt. And 'cause it's the natural way of things, he'll come to see that in time."

"Time . . . what I need most and have none of," Blair replied despondently. She looked into her grandmother's solemn face, unaware of the desperation that clouded her own. "He's sworn to fight me for Danny. He still believes that I'm the cause of Luke's death and wants his revenge." An empty laugh escaped Blair's trembling lips. "Ironic, isn't it? He wants to punish me for what was probably the kindest act I ever committed." Her chin quivered slightly, but then set with a persevering tilt. "Danny will not be another innocent casualty in Matt's and my private war. I won't let Matt hurt him in his attempt to destroy me."

"Those ere powerful words—revenge, hurt, destroy. Ere you so sure that Matt hates you so much and loves Danny so little?"

Blair looked away from her grandmother and stared out onto the hills. The edge of night slowly pulled its velvet curtain over the tranquil sky, filling the mountain gaps and blanketing the valley. "Why can't things be as simple for me as they are for you, Grams?" she groaned. "The basics you preached were easy enough—live by the Bible, stand by your man, and never turn your back on a friend. Yet the peace that comforts you eludes me." Grams sensed the resigned sigh she had smothered.

"It's all in the words, honey—basics, the simple life. You never could content yourself with that. I ain't condemnin' you for it. I'm just saying that dissatisfaction ofttimes breeds grief."

"Believe me, Grams, when I tell you that it wasn't the material things I craved. It was the recognition of being treated as an equal." Blair's grave voice trembled. "It was pride, Grams . . . foolish pride and something more . . ." Unconsciously her yearning gaze scanned the closing darkness. "It was the burning want for an uncommon man," she admitted. "And it's always been in vain."

The monotonous creak of the rocker resumed, but the old woman held her tongue.

CHAPTER THREE

A semi-ferocious shriek of "Geronimo-ooo!" filled the still afternoon air. With a daring leap and flailing legs, Danny swung on the hemp rope out over the "dippin' spring," then toppled to the swirling water below. Since the supreme test of courage had been successfully attempted at least thirty times previously, Blair's concern was muted, along with her praise of the feat. This time when her son's head bobbed above the water, she merely waved a silent acknowledgment. Chagrined by his mother's waning enthusiasm, Danny shook his wet curls like a drenched puppy and paddled aimlessly about while contriving a new ploy for attention.

Blair reached for the bottle of suntan oil. Keeping a vigilant eye on her impetuous son's activities, she began to smooth the oil over her long legs. She'd always tried to mask her obsessive protectiveness of Danny, never wanting to stifle his youthful curiosity or his adventurous nature. Although she herself had swung from that ancient oak many times in her rash youth, she couldn't help but remember the bottomless curse of the "dippin' spring"— those who'd discovered its fathomless depth had never surfaced to brag on it. So she watched, discreetly but guardedly, as Danny paddled to shore and began his ascent of the rocky ledge where the sprawling oak stood.

With an unconscious motion she spread the glistening

oil over her bare shoulders and across the firm cleavage that peeked above her strapless swimsuit. All the while, from beneath a delicate veil of auburn lashes, she observed the supple form of a miniature Matt climbing to the top of the bluff. How much he favored his father, not obviously, but prospectively—the confidence with which he climbed, the aggressiveness of his pursuit. The bottle of suntan oil dropped onto the picnic blanket. She sat up straighter, shading her eyes against the bright sunlight while gazing thoughtfully upward at the agile replica of Matt . . . her child . . . his heir . . . their son.

Pleased that he'd regained his mother's undivided attention, Danny beamed down at her from the summit. Then, beating his small chest King Kong fashion, he gave an echoing Tarzan yodel, charged the rope, swung, and plunged feet first into the fathomless depths. Seconds later a breaking splash revealed his mopsy red head and impish grin. Blair exhaled the breath she hadn't even realized she'd been holding.

"I think the turtles would appreciate your taking a rest, Danny. Why don't you come out for a while and we'll try some of Grams's fried chicken?"

"Awww, not now, Mom," he shouted back breathlessly, ducking like a porpoise back under the water to avoid being beached.

With a sigh Blair stretched back upon her elbows and followed his small figure as he swam about the watering hole. A pliable twig, she thought, in our hands so easily bent or, God forbid, snapped in two. The undisciplined thought caused anxious bands to tighten about her chest. Unwillingly Blair returned to the dilemma she'd been struggling with all during the torturous night—how to dissuade Matt from the disastrous course he'd set upon? During those long, fitful hours when sleep was denied her she had pondered what action to take. *Try reason,* she'd told herself, *appeal to any shred of sensitivity he might still have.* But could she depend on that? Could she put any faith in an inherent, still unrecognized paternal instinct to protect his offspring? Especially when Matt's irrational hatred of her transcended all other emotions? A shimmer of unshed tears momentarily distorted her view of her son.

"Hello, there," a distant voice called out, causing Blair's head to swivel from the water to the high trail. Jim Akins's lean figure appeared from amid the tangled foliage, his minister's tether unsnapped and golden head shining in the sun.

"Afternoon," she called back, glancing from his lanky approach to Danny, still frolicking in the water, until a rustle in the thicket told her he was beside her.

"And a beautiful afternoon it is!" He smiled broadly, easing himself onto a corner of the blanket and handing her a hastily picked spray of wildflowers. "Compliments of Mother Nature," he quipped as she delicately examined the blossoms. His indigo eyes relinquished her, turning out onto the water and Danny's cavorting antics. "Now I'd say that's a frugal lad who doesn't waste one precious moment of a splendid day. A carefree specimen if ever I've seen one!"

"It's when he stops being carefree and becomes careless that worries me," she complained, her hazel eyes narrowing as Danny's head surfaced only inches short of a jutting rock.

"He only suffers from the eagerness of youth, Blair," Jim said soothingly, but he kept a steady eye on the boy himself. "There'll be time enough for caution in the life to come. It's a disadvantage we adults cultivate."

"Among others," she responded before catching herself.

"Yes, among others," he affirmed in a mild voice as he turned to face her again. "And what of the shepherd mother? Is she enjoying the hills as much as her wayward lamb?" Though the words were spoken lightly, his probing look was darker and more serious.

Uncomfortably Blair's gaze deserted him, first traveling to Danny, and then dropping to study the posy in her hand. "Of course," she affirmed, smiling faintly when she looked up. "Need you ask?"

"Yes," he answered flatly, his soul-searching eyes remaining fixed upon her. "I wonder when one leaves these hills and is introduced to such sophistication, if it's possible to reacclimate yourself? Seldom does anything remain just as we remember it."

"Your inaccurate picture of my life-style flatters me, Reverend," she purposely hedged. "You've heard the old saying about taking the hillbilly out of the hills, but never the hills out of the hillbilly. Actually I never expected to find everything exactly as I left it. In fact, in some ways I'd hoped not to."

Jim folded his legs Indian-fashion and idly twiddled a buttercup resting beside his knee. Blair shaded her eyes once more, watching Danny's ascent to the mammoth oak.

"And were those hopes realized, Blair?" Jim quietly asked as he, too, trained his eyes on the young daredevil who stalked the bluff.

51

"No . . . but I didn't have to tell you that, did I?" She cast him a brief but penetrating glance.

"No, you didn't," he admitted.

Blair seemed to discount his presence entirely as she stared up at her son and continued. "Farrett's Corner is eternal—eternally rooted, unified, and terse."

"You say it with the same conviction as a fire and brimstone preacher on the subject of eternal damnation."

An odd smile curved her full mouth. "Maybe so, Reverend. Around here, I'm not sure you can separate the two." Her back arched as Danny took another run at the dangling rope. When he removed a hand to wave at her in midair, she sprang to her feet. The boy's grip slipped, sending him toppling prematurely into shallower water with a smacking belly flop. Blair lurched in concern, but Jim's restraining touch upon her leg delayed her anxious reaction.

"He's all right, Blair. An occasional belly flop is to be expected."

As he spoke Danny's welcomed face emerged above the surface, an embarrassed sputter preceding a grandstand display of his perfected backstroke. With an unconscious sigh Blair eased back upon the blanket. She, too, felt a flush of embarrassment, partly due to her overreaction, partly because of the obvious way in which Jim Akins was studying her. It made her slightly uneasy to share such casual circumstances with a minister—the cozy setting, the scanty attire, the unspoken camaraderie which passed between them.

"Rev Akins . . ." The title barely passed her lips when he broke in.

"Since I was gallant enough not to step on your toes the other evening, I insist you call me Jim."

"Jim . . ." She smiled uncertainly. "As much as I enjoy your company, I think it's only fair to warn you of the consequences of being seen in mine. I wouldn't win any popularity contest in Farrett's Corner. An association with me, no matter how innocent, could mar your reputation."

A somber expression crept over his candid face. "I appreciate your concern and the warning, Blair, but I'm a man who forms his own opinions and lives his own life. It happens that I find you refreshing and intriguing company."

Now she was studying him. His strange choice of words added to her disquiet. "Intriguing," she repeated, casting a quick look at Danny before returning her attention to him. "A curious word for you to use to describe me."

"Why does it surprise you?" His blue eyes glimmered with true bewilderment.

Blair felt a twinge of apprehension. "To be honest, it sounds a bit worldly for a man of the cloth."

"But you see, Blair, like you, I'm made up of many facets." He nodded at Danny. "I, too, am a mother's son, another struggling mortal, a friend to those who'd allow me. It's true that I'm foremost a servant of God, but I'm also a man, and it's the man who finds you intriguing."

Her complete astonishment at his bluntness caused a flip remark to blurt from her lips. "Are you certain it isn't just the outcast's soul that interests you?"

He merely smiled, kindly and knowingly. "And are you so uncomfortable with a passing compliment?"

A tense second passed between them before Blair's pensive face broke out in a similar smile. "Not normally," she conceded.

"Then we're even, because I don't normally give them." He grinned wide, inviting her admiring nod and musical laughter.

"Hey, Mom! Who's that with you?" Danny's inquisitive voice floated back from the willows at the edge of the spring.

Blair cupped her hands to her mouth, replying, "A friend of mine. And your time's up, nosy polliwog!"

"Just one more jump, please," he begged, churning the water to stay afloat.

"No more today. Now, come on out of there. If we don't eat every bite of Grams's chicken, we don't dare go home." Her tactic worked, and Danny swam for shore. She reached for the picnic basket with a persuasive smile. "There's plenty, Jim. Won't you stay and share with Danny and me?"

Cocking his golden head to one side, he pretended to consider the invitation for a moment. Then, with an exaggerated drawl and mischievous grin, he trapped her. "I'd be delighted, Mrs. Hayden, provided that you and Danny agree to be my guests at the church's annual catfish fry next Saturday night."

Blair's tug at the picnic basket was impeded by Jim Akins' firm hand on the opposite end of the handle. Their eyes met, her silent demur overruled by his gentle appeal.

"We'd be honored," she reluctantly agreed, against her better judgment.

Twisting her hair into a French knot at the base of her neck, Blair secured the arrangement with two ornate combs and then leaned to check her reflection in the mirror. She straightened the collar of her mauve blouse, primped the crease in her slacks, and critically fluffed the copper wisps that framed her sun-tinted cheeks. At last the image before her passed inspection. She flipped off the lightswitch and left the bedroom, her soft footsteps trailing to the end of the hall. There they paused as she eased open the door to peek in on Danny. He lay in deep sleep, an exhausted snore floating from his slack mouth and the bed sheets tangled about his firm little thighs. With careful steps and a gentle touch, Blair straightened the covers and patted his sleeping head. Then, kissing his cheek, she eased out of the room and silently pulled the door to.

As she proceeded on into what Grams called the "sittin' room" another snore, lower and gravelly, greeted her. Grams sat slumped in her favorite chair, swollen feet propped upon a footstool, her silver head crooked in the cranny of the wingback, and her embroidery lying deserted in her lap. In repose the deep lines that etched her woodsy face appeared less strained, and her gnarled hands, the product of endless hours of toil, lay at ease and graceful. With a feather-light motion, Blair retrieved the neglected embroidery piece and deposited it upon the stone ledge of the hearth. Then, shaking out a coverlet that lay folded beside the wood bin, she gently spread it over Grams's gouty legs. One more kiss, this time upon a withered cheek, and Blair padded across the braided rug to slip out the screen door.

The humid night air engulfed her. A scent of rain loomed heavily, and intermittent streaks of light cut through the summer sky. The tension in the air matched her mood, charged and volatile. Blair couldn't help thinking that if all did not go well in the next hour or so they would be weeping together. Another bolt of energy flashed across the skyline, silhouetting the undulating terrain that surrounded the valley. Blair stood mesmerized for a thoughtful moment, reminded of the power that lay waiting in those hills—Farrett power, a force to be respected, yet a threat she must deal with. Quickly she removed her keys from her slacks pocket, as if this action would stiffen her courage. Then, walking purposefully toward the Ferrari, she started psyching herself up for the encounter ahead. No matter what passed between Matt and herself during this impromptu visit, she had to be firm and victorious. *For Danny's sake,* she thought. *For all of our sakes . . . For pity's sake, please, just this once, let me win!*

Brilliant threads of lightning mazed the ebony sky. Beneath their staccato glare the treetops swayed in the mounting winds. In the stables behind Farrett House the horses flinched in their stalls, their ears pinned back and eyes wild with alarm. With crooning words and soothing pats Matt moved from stall to stall, trying to calm the high-strung animals. "Easy, Desperado, easy," he said soothingly, stroking the flared nostrils of a sleek Arabian. Nervously the stallion's hooves pranced in place upon the dirt floor.

A gust of wind banged the stable door shut, causing the filly in the end stall to rear in fright. The most skittish of all, her spooked whinny accompanied the frenetic pounding of her hind hooves against the wall. "It's all right, temperamental lady," Matt assured her, cautiously approaching the high-spirited filly. At the sound of his voice her platinum-maned head jerked upright, and she began to bump the the sides of the stall with her trim haunches. Slowly Matt eased a steadying hand toward her. The fickle female shied from his advance, rearing again.

"You still need to learn an easier hand with a filly, Matt." Blair's melodious voice startled him. He spun toward the sound. She was standing only a few feet away, hands thrust into her pockets and one shoulder braced against the barn door.

"What in the hell are you doing here, Blair?" he growled.

At first she didn't reply as she slowly strolled past him toward the filly. "Whoa, pretty red," she droned in a lullaby chant. "A little wind, a little light, that's all, girl." Reassuringly her hand stroked the filly's slender neck. The agitated swaying ceased, a relaxed shudder rippling down her flanks. Blair's hand continued to work its magic. She pressed her cheek to the silky-coated neck for a moment, and then raised her eyes to Matt's. For a brief second his gaze held unguarded admiration. Her velvet words had half-hypnotized him also, he had to exert a mental effort to shake himself clear. Instantly the glow within his eyes diminished as his perturbed expression returned. He was about to repeat his demand for an explanation when Blair willingly offered one.

"I want to talk about Danny, Matt. It's important!" In the dim lamplight the green of her eyes shaded as mauve as her blouse. Matt's hostility was tempered by their mellowness.

"I think any discussions we have about Danny should be done through our lawyers."

"That's why I'm here, Matt. I hoped that we could avoid a lengthy and bitter court battle where the only one

57

who really stands to lose is Danny." She retreated from the calmed filly, replacing her hands in her pockets and pacing back to the barn door to blend with the shadows once more.

Matt's steely gaze followed her. "Since you've yet to even admit the Farrett bloodline, what other options do I have?"

"And if I were willing to concede the fact, just that and nothing else, would you stop this madness?" The strain in her voice became evident. She slumped back against the door frame for support.

"No!" In a dismissive manner Matt cast a final glance over his stock before moving toward the door. Then, as if having second thoughts, he paused only inches short of her. "You still don't understand, do you? I don't want a public admission; I want Danny! Get a lawyer, Blair, and while you're at it get a good one. Believe me, you'll need him." He threw open the stable door, marching past her without a backward glance.

Impulsively Blair chased after him, down the cobblestone path and across the perfectly manicured lawn. The mounting storm winds riled about them as her hand reached out and clutched his shirt sleeve. "Will you do this at any cost? Are you so filled with hate, Matt, that you'd destroy a happy little boy?" Strain had turned to desperation as she stood pleading and clinging to his arm.

When Matt saw her drawn face, he couldn't help but feel a twinge of compassion. God knew he didn't want to feel it. In fact, when it came to Blair Logan, he wished he were totally immune. "What is it you want, Blair?" he sighed. "For me to step aside gracefully so as not complicate your orderly life? I won't forfeit my claim on Danny.

to spare you embarrassment! No, I won't stand on the sidelines and watch you make fools of the Farretts once again!"

"Oh, Matt, why won't you listen to me?" she groaned. "Don't you see it has nothing to do with us or the past? It's Danny and his future I'm concerned with. What must I do to make you understand how devastating this could be to him? He's an innocent child who'll be caught in the middle of our grudge match."

A peal of thunder clapped overhead. Matt's gaze lifted to the sweeping clouds that raced to obscure the moon. "The storm's moving in fast. Go home, Blair." He made a move to leave, but her anxious fingers tightened about his arm.

"All right, Matt, let's strike a bargain. If you'll drop this custody suit, I'll work out an arrangement for us to share Danny." A strong gust of wind carried her promise to his unsuspecting ears, and then tossed it out into the black emptiness that surrounded them.

For the longest time, with only the howl of the wind and the rumble of distant thunder in the background, Matt stared down at her. Could it be that her only motivation was to protect her son from getting hurt? Could a woman like Blair care that much for anyone? Or was it just a dramatic means of getting what she'd always wanted—her own way? If so, she deserved an Academy Award for this performance. Her acting ability had improved greatly since last they'd clashed.

"No deal, Blair," he quietly declined. "Now, if you'll excuse me . . ." Again, he attempted to take his leave.

"Damn you, Matthew Farrett!" Now her fingernails bit

into his flesh as she detained him. "Why must you persist with this insanity?" she cried hysterically.

"For one good reason, Blair," he answered calmly. "I don't trust you, and I never strike bargains with people I don't trust."

Even though his explanation was not totally unexpected, the apathetic manner in which he delivered it numbed her. "I see. So you're still convinced that I'm an unscrupulous opportunist who'd use any means to get what I wanted?"

There was no reply, only his stony look looming in judgment over her.

"Even if what you assume about me was true, Matt, don't you believe that people can change?" She raised her searching eyes to his, her chin set, but it was the slight tremble of her pouty lips that captured his attention.

Reflexively his palm cupped that prideful chin, his thumb lightly tracing the outline of her seductive mouth. "Have you changed so much, Blair?" he coaxed, his intent blue eyes lingering on her lips.

"Yes . . . I . . ." She stumbled as his other hand began to travel suggestively up her arm.

"Then a man's touch doesn't stir you as it once did? You don't yearn to be petted more?" Deliberately his roaming hand slid up her neck as his fingers nimbly removed the combs that secured her hair, freeing the lustrous strands to tumble down her back.

Blair experienced both panic and confusion. His contact ignited dangerous feelings that impaired any rational thinking on her part. How she had longed to have him touch her like this. How many endless nights had she lain awake, wishing for this moment? But those dreamed-of advances lacked warmth in reality. Matt's seductive touch felt premeditated and mechanical. This she could sense, and this she feared.

"Stop it, Matt," she entreated, twisting her head to avoid the titillating fingers that stroked her hair.

"Ahhh, then you have changed. The Blair Logan I remember wouldn't have told a man to stop." His hand caressed the thick silk of her hair before methodically beginning to massage her narrow back. In a swift motion his arm yoked about her waist, his body pressing intimately nearer. Just as swiftly sensual impulses surged through Blair. She could barely distinguish Matt's words above the deafening pounding of her heart. "By now Blair Logan's body would beg to be embraced, and her lips would deliver a silent invitation—just as yours are doing at this moment." His hand still cradled her chin, and his thumb continued its relentless teasing of her lips. What had begun as a cruel taunt had now expanded beyond his control. Caught up in his own perverse game, he had no choice but to play it through, though to win the contest, he might very well deplete the limited reserve of willpower he'd maintained.

"Are you crazy, Matt?" he heard her whisper. "What are you trying to prove?" She pressed the flat of her hands against his chest, trying to escape his viselike hold. A light mist began to rain down upon them. The wind swirled about their linked forms and ruffled their damp hair. A glare of lightning lit the sky, followed by an angry clap of thunder that resounded from hill to hill in an encircling relay. In the light of that brilliant flash Blair read the merciless purpose in his dazed eyes, and she began to lash out wildly to break free of his trap.

Matt grabbed her wrists, yanking them around his waist to the small of his back and holding her prisoner against his hard form. Her breath was labored, her soft breasts expanding, then waning upon his sensitive chest. The excitement in her expressive eyes flashed like the energized heavens. Before Matt could stop himself, his mouth claimed hers, his heart racing like the wind and pounding like thunder. He tightened his hold, crushing her closer, his mouth pursuing hers as she attempted to maneuver away from his demanding onslaught. But when his tongue parted her lips to explore and fondle the sweeter recesses beyond, she moaned beneath his passionate advance, ceased her struggling, and melted against his solid support. He released her wrists, only to find her arms encircling his back and drawing him even nearer to her provocative body. Her returning ardor obliterated all of his original purpose from his mind. Helplessly he discovered himself suffocating in a vacuum of desire. Somehow, not knowing from where, he found the strength to clutch her shoulders and withdraw from her petal-soft mouth.

During that long, consuming kiss the rains grew steadier, but neither Matt nor Blair were conscious of it. Beneath Matt's strong hands and fiery gaze Blair's blouse clung transparently to her bare breasts. For a dull instant Matt seemed unaware of all else except the tempting, taut centers which showed darkly through the sheer material. He felt the shudder of unfulfilled need that passed through her slim body, and, suddenly, he snapped back to his senses.

His plan had backfired. He had meant to expose the Blair he'd vowed to loathe. Instead he had only managed to reveal his own weakness for her. Matt knew he must

hide the truth from her. For the sake of the Farrett name
. . . for pride's sake . . . For his own sanity, this time he
had to win out over her.

Again he trailed the curve of her lips with a fingertip,
but this time his body language took on an insulting tone.
"You see, Blair, you haven't changed so much," he taunted. "You're still a desirable woman . . . still desirable, easy,
treacherous. Try convincing someone else that you've re-
formed, because your talents are wasted on me."

She cringed from his cruel barb, the back of her hand
striking away his compelling touch. For the first time she
felt the chill of the wind and the rain. And something
more . . . the cold vastness of Matthew's hatred. Abuse
was all he would willingly offer her, now or ever.

Pretending to only wipe at the raindrops collected on
her cheeks, she brushed away the tears that stung her eyes.
"You think you've proved something, Matt. Well, in a
way I guess you have. From here on out it's winner take
all and no quarter given." Strands of wet hair whipped
about her stricken face, emphasizing the golden fire sparkling in her eyes. "I've only one other thing to say to you,
Matthew Farrett. I may be a long way from perfect, but
I'm not nearly as sorry as you!" Once she had said her
piece, Blair fled from the hurtful sight of him. Blindly she
ran through the hazy rain until she reached the sanctity
of her Ferrari.

With a flip of the ignition, the sportscar tore through
the main gates of Farrett House, accelerating even faster
once she was out on the winding gravel lane. The rain
pelted against the windshield, mingling with the rhythmic
thump of the wipers and Blair's soft sobs. Steadily the
speedometer climbed, the precision-engineered Ferrari

taking the steep curves at a reckless clip. Overcome by depression, Blair never saw the fork in the road until it loomed only perilous yards ahead. At the last possible moment her foot hit the brake. The Ferrari fishtailed, stopping only a few feet shy of a dividing gully. Traumatized, she shifted into park and collapsed upon the steering wheel, her legs shaking and her mind spinning.

"You're a fool . . . just like Matt said, you're a fool," she moaned aloud, her head rocking involuntarily against the wheel. "Why did you risk coming back here?"

Numbly she leaned her head back against the seat, listening to the droning idle of the motor and collecting herself. Her reasons were complicated and many, and she'd never deceived herself that achieving her objective would be easy. Yet the one possibility she hadn't considered was Matt's instinctive obsession with Danny. Throughout her life her ability to cope had sustained her, and it would again. At least one of her goals would be accomplished—the acquisition of Farrett Mines by Hayden Petroleum. Of this she was certain.

Wiping the tearstains from her cheeks, Blair sat erect. Self-pity was an indulgence she seldom permitted herself. She hadn't the time or energy to spare. With Danny's security at stake she must act decisively. With a resolute click the Ferrari jumped into gear, heading back toward the Hollow. Minutes later it pulled up beside the barn, and Blair ran for cover beneath the cedar shakes of the back porch. Drained, she slumped in Grams's wicker rocker to stare out at the gray veil of rain.

She'd hadn't returned to Farrett's Corner as the naive and ineffectual woman she'd once been. Exposure to a world beyond these hills and Jess's guidance had tutored her in the fine art of overpowering the opposition. For over a year she'd carefully prepared to bring about this merger. Though she'd hoped not to be forced into the position of having to bring financial pressure to bear, Matt's stubborn refusal of her offer, coupled with his threat of a custody suit, left her no choice. She was no newcomer to power plays. A capable and diligent pupil, she'd studied strategy with a master—her husband, Jess. Often he'd told her, "The one thing that powerful men respect above all else is superior power. The wisest always hold it in reserve, and then only use it when it's absolutely necessary."

She closed her eyes and rocked lethargically. No longer did she feel chilled. Somehow the warm security of Jess's influence always affected her like that.

CHAPTER FOUR

"Mr. Hershell will be with you shortly, Mrs. Hayden." The prim receptionist smiled stiffly, then motioned for Blair to take a seat upon the Mayflower bench outside the vice-president's door. "Would you care for a cup of coffee while you wait?"

"That would be nice. Thank you." Blair settled upon the hard maple, unsnapped her attaché case, and began to sift through the documents inside.

Sensing the receptionist's honed study of her, Blair carefully kept her eyes averted until she heard the woman's fading footsteps upon the terrazzo. Only then did she allow her gaze to wander around the interior of the bank, and only then did she meet the eyes of Steven Bishop. He looked every bit the part he'd been playing for six months—a modest accountant, tucked away in an inconspicuous corner. They exchanged meaningful glances a tense second before the returning tap of the receptionist's high heels forced them to turn and break contact.

"I forgot to ask if you took cream or sugar. I have some in my desk drawer," the receptionist said distractedly.

"Black is just fine." Blair's response was as mechanical as her acceptance of the proffered paper cup. The woman hesitated, her hawk eyes tarrying over the documents resting on Blair's lap.

"Will Mr. Hershell be much longer?" Blair's commanding tone reclaimed the woman's attention. With a pointed gesture she turned the paperwork face down on her lap.

The receptionist's tense smile stretched to a thin slit. Though clearly miffed, she was wise enough to remember her position. "I can check if you like," she retorted coolly.

"Please do." Blair's eyes dismissed her.

As the woman huffed back to her desk, Blair turned her papers over and studied their vital contents. With each sip of her coffee she checked to be certain that the receptionist maintained her distance. At this crucial stage she had no intention of allowing some snoopy clerk a peek at the confidential report which had been so painstakingly compiled.

As she read the incriminating facts before her, her thoughts wandered once more to Steven Bishop across the room. How long and diligently he had worked to give her this edge she needed. Steven was one of her most trusted employees at Hayden Petroleum. Not only was he conscientious, but extremely thorough. She'd known all along that if there had been any indiscretions at Farrett Mercantile, Steven would uncover all the details. Her hunch had paid off. Now, on the threshold of accomplishing their objective, Blair had to curb an impulse to give Bishop a sign, *Well done.*

"Mr. Hershell can see you now." The receptionist rose to open the austere oak doors.

Hurriedly stuffing her paperwork back inside the attaché case, Blair silently followed. Once she had stepped into the anteroom, she was immediately struck by the pompous opulence that surrounded her. *In character,* she mused as the dapper figure seated behind the executive desk got to his feet.

"I'm sorry to have kept you waiting, Mrs. Hayden. Please, have a seat." Mason Hershell's smile was as thin as his apology.

"That's quite all right, Mr. Hershell. I know how busy you must be. I'm grateful that you could see me at all on such short notice." Passing her half-empty coffee cup to the lingering receptionist, Blair, again, gave her a nod of dismissal.

"That'll be all for the moment, Miss Ferguson." Hershell waited for her to close the door as Blair took up a position directly opposite him in front of the desk.

An insubordinate slam of the door produced an embarrassed snort from the vice-president. "Well, now, Mrs. Hayden . . ." He resumed his seat, and his voice took on an expectant tone. "In what way can Farrett Mercantile be of service to you?" His preying eyes evaluated his unexpected caller. He liked the cut of her clothes, well-tailored and fashionable. Everything about her spoke of wealth—from the fine white linen suit she wore to the tasteful accessories, cultured pearls and black leather pumps.

"I've come to seek your assistance in acquiring a local business I'm interested in, Mr. Hershell." Blair crossed one slender leg over the other and shot him her most beguiling smile. Little did he realize he was being led down the primrose path.

Mason's gaze fell for a brief instant to her shapely legs. At the moment he didn't know which intrigued him more —her shady past or the substantial account she represented in the future. Quickly greed overcame lust, and he raised his eyes to her attractive face.

"I've acquainted myself with Hayden Petroleum's holdings, Mrs . . ." He improvised a charming smile. "May I call you Blair?" he asked in a solicitous voice.

"Certainly, Mason," she agreed sweetly.

A smug look flitted across his face as he realized how easily he was manipulating her. This frivolous heiress was going to be like putty in his hands. "As I was saying, Blair, once I realized exactly who you were I took the liberty of acquainting myself with the extent of your holdings. Actually I wanted to be prepared for just such a contingency as this so that I—" He abruptly corrected himself. "Rather, I mean, we, Farrett Mercantile, might accommodate you in some way."

"How perceptive and thoughtful of you, Mason," she cooed, but in her mind she was seething, *And how very predictable.* The private investigator she'd hired had done his job well. Mason Hershell was as inept as he was corrupt. She hoped the rest of the investigative background report proved to be as accurate. She'd banked on the fact that his father was as obsessed with protecting the family honor as Mason was at abusing it.

Being very pleased with himself thus far, Mason missed the golden glint that hardened her eyes as she reached for her attaché case. Instead he was lulled into a reverie by her feline movements. This was one sexy number. Even though the wide-brimmed straw hat she wore partially hid her sultry features, the way she moved was unmistakably sensual. He found himself daydreaming about unbinding her hair from the tight coil at the back of her neck, then he imagined himself running his hands through that shining auburn mane. He had just begun to mentally undress her when he realized she was speaking to him.

"I've had my staff prepare this preliminary report on

the company in question. I believe that after you examine it, you'll understand exactly what sort of assistance I'll need from you. . . ." She paused meaningfully, then corrected herself as she passed him a manila folder. "Clumsy of me. Of course, I meant to say from Farrett Mercantile."

Flattered and completely fooled, the opportunistic Hershell rushed to assure her. "Not at all, Blair. We're one and the same." His hand lingered as he accepted the proposal.

"I hope so, Mason," she said softly, slowly shrinking from his repulsive touch.

The cocky banker settled back in his chair to study the report. His eyes had only scanned the first paragraph when his fingers visibly tightened their grip on the pages. He drew the document closer to better examine it. Slowly the insipid smile faded from his lips as he looked up at Blair, then back at the report in utter disbelief. There came a nervous clearing of his throat before he attempted to speak.

"It says here that the company in question is Farrett Mines." At her silent nod of acknowledgment Hershell's amiable expression disappeared altogether. "You can't be serious?"

"Oh, but I am, Mason," she drawled.

Something in her tone made him uneasy. He set the report aside, as if already vetoing the entire matter. "I'm afraid you've been misinformed, Mrs. Hayden." He had purposely reverted to a formal mode of address. "The acquisition of Farrett Mines is out of the question."

"I think not, Mason," she insisted, a faint smile stealing across her full lips. "I happen to know that your bank holds a lien on the mine—a second mortgage taken out for

70

the purpose of expansion and modernization. It's all in the report, Mason. Please, read on."

Her superior attitude galled him. Suddenly he preferred not to pursue this conversation any longer. Rising to his feet, he attempted to hand back the sheaf of papers. "I'm sorry to tell you that at this time Farrett Mercantile has no desire to sell the note, Mrs. Hayden. It's an interesting proposition, but, I'm afraid, totally out of the question. Now, unless there is something else you wished to discuss . . ." He tactfully inclined his head toward the door.

Tired of the game, Blair's eyes snapped as she leaned forward in her chair. "I've given you an ultimatum, Mason, not a proposition. Now sit down and pay attention to what I have to say."

Hershell stiffened at the insult. "I beg your pardon?" he said coldly.

"I *said*, be seated and be still." she repeated sternly. Then, pointing to the report he'd discarded, she ignored his stunned look and continued. "Now, Mason, we both know that it is a legitimate practice for lending institutions to sell corporate notes at a profit. With money being as tight as it is, actually it's just plain good business." Literally speechless, the banker eased back into his overstuffed chair and stared at her.

"If you had bothered to read the fine print, you'd see that I'm offering more than a fair price. It's a sound proposal which I expect you to put before the board, as well as to endorse personally." With a challenging look she nudged the pages in his direction, then sat back casually in her chair.

"This is absurd!" he scoffed. "If I didn't know better, I'd think you were threatening me."

"How very astute of you, Mason." The positive timbre of her voice caused his pulse to quicken. *Maybe he'd underestimated the lady? Could it be that she was cleverer than he'd first thought?* She reached into her briefcase once more, and then tossed a second folder atop his desk. His fingers hesitated as for the first time he noted the cunning animation in her green cat's eyes. It was as if she had dared him to open Pandora's box.

"Is this supposed to convince me?" He tried to feign indifference, but his fingers worked a nervous tap upon the folder.

"If it doesn't, you're even more reckless than I thought." She leveled a steady gaze at him, leaned back, and awaited his inspection.

The heading on the stationery gave him his first clue— *Stone and Bruell, Private Investigators.* Beads of perspiration began to dot his forehead as he read the underlined caption of the report—background and surveillance of one Mason Lawrence Hershell. He loosened his tie and undid the top button of his shirt. The longer he skimmed over the incriminating evidence mounting against him, the more he labored for air.

"You've been a naughty boy, Mason." Blair's accusation jolted his head upright. "Dipping into the till to cover up your personal losses was foolish, not to mention illegal. What amazes me most is that you've gotten away with it for so long."

At that strained moment the intercom on the vice-president's desk buzzed. Mason jammed his finger on the button, growling, "I thought I told you to hold all calls, Miss Ferguson."

"But, sir, it's Hershell Senior, and he says it's urgent."

"Take a message."

"But, sir—" the receptionist persisted.

"Damnit, Ferguson! Are you deaf? I said take a message." The snap of the intercom button cut off the receptionist's gasp.

"Daddy's going to be upset with you, Mason," Blair said smoothly as Hershell jerked the handkerchief from his pocket and mopped his brow. "Especially when he finds out that you've been misappropriating funds."

"That sounds very close to blackmail, Mrs. Hayden." Red blotches began to appear at the base of Mason's neck.

"Not at all," Blair assured him. "I'd prefer to call it guaranteed cooperation. Since your father is the majority stockholder in this bank and the chairman of the board, I'm sure he'll support your recommendation to sell the Farrett Mines note. After all, he's the one who insisted on making you a vice-president. With the family honor at stake he'll simply have no choice."

Blair rose from her chair, retrieved the private investigator's report from his desk, and put it back inside her attaché case. "I'll take this with me and leave the Hayden offer in your capable hands. Do I make myself clear, Mason?"

"Perfectly," he seethed, the red splotches climbing his neck to spot his cheeks.

"I'll expect a signed contract in a few days. It's been a pleasure, Mason." Blair swung her attaché case to her left hand and held out her right.

"You're a ruthless woman, aren't you? Cold as ice." Mason glared his contempt and ignored her hand.

Blair merely shrugged her shoulders, answering evenly,

73

"It's a quality that you most certainly should recognize, Mason," before making for the door.

A week later found Blair patiently waiting once more—this time for the evening whistle at the mines and a showdown with Matt. As she watched the weary miners, grimed with the sweat and dust of the land, begin the homeward trek, she remembered Mason's parting words, *Ruthless . . . cold as ice. Maybe hard times, hard lives, made for hard people,* she thought. Maybe, like these solemn men, she was the joint product of heredity and environment—a hickory hillbilly fighting just to stay alive?

Absently her fingers smoothed the leather attaché case. Inside it were the mortgage assignment documents she'd demanded from Mason Hershell—the power with which to neutralize Matt. Her intentions were ruthless, her resolve unshakable, yet her conscience bore the burden of her willfulness. Blair hated the thought of compromising a man's pride, of bartering heritage for custody. For both were priceless and nonnegotiable. Why did fate always dictate that she and Matt must hurt each other?

Blair shifted her weight uncomfortably on the car seat, then lifted her hair from her neck to catch a breath of breeze. As she waited for the caravan of vehicles to file out of the parking lot and trickle down the mountain, her eyes absently scanned the horizon. The day's oppressive heat collected in the copper sky and with the barest of whispers the sinewy cottonwoods rustled their relief. Unlike the appreciative cottonwood, Blair knew that evening would bring more than just a reprieve from the heat; it would also bring her guilt and Matt's submission. The last pickup cleared the gates and meandered down the mountain.

74

Only Matt's familiar Cherokee remained in the parking lot. Blair started the Ferrari's motor and eased out from her observation post off Miner's Road. She passed through the gates, parked beside the Cherokee, and stepped out of the car, briefcase in hand.

The outer offices were simply furnished and, more importantly, deserted. Blair's mind dwelled on a significant detail as she forced her hesitant steps forward—*Matt's* consideration of other people's pride. He did not flaunt his superiority before those whom he must, at times, impose it on. These were working offices, not showrooms. A bang of a file cabinet drawer from behind a half-open door at the end of the hall induced an apprehensive lurch within Blair's chest. She never broke stride. She had the feeling that if she stopped now, her will, as well as her cause, would be lost. *God!* How she dreaded this moment. With a nudge against the door, she entered unseen and unheard into Matt's domain.

He stood with his back to her, engrossed in a file folder in his hands, a broad shoulder braced against the file cabinet, shirt sleeves rolled up. The evening's bronze light streaming through the slatted venetian blinds highlighted his powerful figure. He appeared taller and more virile than she'd ever recalled. A crazy vision leapt into her head—of herself tiptoeing over and slowly sliding her palms about his slim waist, then grazing them across his firm abdomen in silent homage, pressing her cheek against the muscular expanse of his back to feel the ripple of excitement coursing through him. Then he would turn to take her within his sheltering arms, folding her close—so close that they breathed as one until his soft, delivering

75

kiss transported her beyond the tops of the cottonwoods to bask in the heavens' copper glow . . .

"Blair?" The hazy vision dissipated at the sound of her name. Matt stood staring at her curiously, and for a humiliating moment she wondered if he could read her mind. But as he slung the file folder onto his desk and tiredly rubbed the back of his neck his tone assured her otherwise. "You never give up, do you?" he sighed.

"No," she replied, equally subdued. "We have to talk, Matt. May I sit down?" Pointedly she trailed her eyes to a chair beside his desk.

"I'd prefer that you didn't. I thought I'd made myself clear, Blair. I'm not changing my position on the custody suit or your barite proposition. Nor am I going to stand here and debate it with you. It's been a long day, and I'm not in the mood to observe social amenities. So, if you wouldn't mind . . ." It was Matt's turn to cast a meaningful glance toward the door. It was also a necessary ploy which allowed him to remove his eyes from her beautiful face. The reality of her was much more difficult to bear than the vision that habitually claimed his dreams.

"Issues are only debatable when one or both parties has an alternative, Matt. Neither of us do." The confident finality in her voice once more caught his attention. He quirked a brow, challenging her to define her intentions. Their battle scars hidden and the skirmish lines drawn, the time had come to attack. Blair's grip on the attaché case tightened, as well as every nerve in her body.

"I now hold the Farrett Mines note." She spoke distinctly and emphatically. "And, make no mistake, unless you agree to certain concessions, I'll have no choice but to foreclose." The words were said, the ultimatum delivered. Though her eyes were set as hard as jade, her heart was wrenched by the pain she witnessed upon his face. He met her unyielding gaze, never perceiving the empathy that lurked behind it.

"So, this is the standoff we've always known would come." His inflections were deliberately calm, as if he no more doubted her veracity than he'd discounted the inevitability of this moment. His only option would be to pay off the note on demand, and to do so would deplete the company's reserves entirely. Even if he won the battle, she'd eventually emerge victorious in the war. And to the victor, Blair Hayden, would go the spoils. Her assumption that there were no alternatives had been correct. His logical mind damned the assumption; his tormented heart, his beloved adversary.

"Yes" was all she could manage, her throat constricting as she watched him slump defeated into a leather chair. She, too, felt the need to sit down before she collapsed beneath the strain. Easing into another chair near his desk, she observed in silence as he lowered his head, then raked his sun-tanned fingers through his hair. A part of her wanted to reach out and clutch those bronze fingertips, draw them to her lips, and kiss away his despair. Yet the hickory hillbilly remembered his fervent vow to claim the son she so fiercely protected. *No one*, not even Matt, had such a right. She'd borne and raised Danny. And never would she allow anyone to separate them.

"It seems as if I should have taken your threat more seriously, 'Winner take all and no quarter given.' Though I'm fairly certain what conditions must be met, for the sake of clarity why don't you define them exactly?" Matt leaned wearily back in his chair, his blue eyes laden with pessimism, the dark circles beneath them more pronounced. Blair fought to remain impassive.

"Your immediate agreement to become Hayden Petroleum's sole barite supplier." She opened her briefcase, retrieved a copy of the preliminary contract, and laid it atop his desk. "A few clauses are negotiable, but these are only minor points." Her eyes lowered to the briefcase as Matt reached for the legal blackmail letter. It was a degrading gesture for him, a grievous one for her. When she'd gained a semblance of self-control, she allowed her gaze to rest on his stony features. A strange sense of pride engulfed her. Even in defeat Matt still commanded her respect.

"After you've had a chance to better examine the contractual terms, you'll find that Hayden Petroleum is offering Farrett Mines lucrative compensation for . . ." His ice blue eyes impaled her, as if to say, "No amount of money could compensate for the usurping of my birthright." The malediction his eyes expressed stabbed at her conscience, but veiling her pain, she continued. "Further, upon signing the final agreement, Hayden Petroleum will transfer to the mine, free and clear title, all debts forgiven, the lien null and void." She felt, rather than saw, the subtle change that crossed his face. Leather creaked as he came erect in his chair.

"I'm a smart enough game player to realize that I lose when my opponent holds a trump card. But experience has also taught me that winners, especially corporate barracudas, are seldom so generous without good reason. Spell out the second condition, Blair!"

Without a flicker of emotion or the slightest hesitation she demanded, "Your written undertaking to drop the

78

custody suit." Her chin rose, her auburn hair swinging back with the abrupt movement. "Together we'll work out a private arrangement by which we share him, but only in the subtlest, smoothest way. Agreed?" There was not a hint of clemency in her brittle voice.

There came a long, unnerving pause as Matt relaxed in his chair, steepled his fingertips over the bridge of his nose, and contemplated her. She moved not a muscle, nor did she retreat from his condescending stare. At last he spoke.

"And if I refuse to comply?"

"I'll take over your company, Matt. I'll break you, and then fight you through every court in this land if I have to, but I'll never concede custody of Danny. I still have as much hill spirit as you. We can resolve this now or feud to our graves. It's entirely up to you."

Gold-flecked eyes locked with crystal blue, neither relenting, neither fully perceiving the full extent of emotion. It was Matt who finally departed from the silent hill code.

"My, but you have grown up, Blair Logan. You're schemes are infinitely more sophisticated and your delivery more poignant."

"Blair Logan had to. Life didn't leave her a choice. Believe it or not, Matt, it's this kind of shabbiness that I'm trying to spare Danny from. Will you agree?" For the first time Matt noted the sadness in her voice, the frail slope of her shoulders. A miserable smirk pulled at the corners of his mouth as he reflected on the irony of his situation. He'd just been pressured into a business arrangement he despised, coerced into forfeiting legal custody of a child he adored, and here he sat, feeling a twinge of pity for his assassin. Somehow, he felt rather like Caesar on the Ides of March.

"You expect me to trust you to be fair about these secret arrangements for Danny?" he mocked.

"You'll have to, Matt" came her resigned pledge as she reached into her attaché case and retrieved the private covenant.

"Before I agree, answer one question. Would you have gone to such drastic lengths just to get the barite?" He watched for a reaction as she rose from her chair. Nothing! Not a clue! The cameo face betrayed no emotion. The fragile shoulders were proudly squared, her graceful carriage unfaltering. Then, as the crucial pact was about to be laid upon his desk, he observed the tremor in her delicate fingers. The paper she was holding actually rattled before it came to rest on his desk to spare her the burden. Instinctively his steady hand pinned hers to the desk. "I deserve an answer, Blair."

Her gaze riveted on his warm, brown hand, she forced a reply through a knot of strangling emotion. "No, Matt. The years haven't corrupted me to such an extent. I would've liked to have persuaded you, but in light of your unwillingness, I most definitely would've looked for barite elsewhere."

His hand lingered for a revealing moment before withdrawing. "Then, I'll agree because, in my own way, I love him, too, Blair." The words came low and difficult, piercing the deepest, most sensitive place in her heart. Salty remorse stung her eyes as she quickly averted her head, clutched the briefcase for support, and then turned to go.

"Today you have the barite and Danny's sole guardianship. But you'd do well to remember that tomorrow is looking over your shoulder." His taunting words trailed her to the door.

Hand on the knob, she hesitated, slowly pivoting to face him. From across the dim room the ache that never allowed her rest went undetected. Yet her voice had a melancholy quality which twilight could not disguise.

"Through the years Blair Logan learned two invaluable lessons, Matt—things are seldom what they seem, and only fools or lovers disregard tomorrow." With a slam of the door he was left to contemplate her meaning.

Rising from his chair, he raised the venetian blinds to stare out over the billowing green of the cottonwoods up at the metallic sky. Far above this feudal world it all looked so serene, so majestic. Up there, unanswerable questions became clear, solutions easy. Why had Blair returned? What had the years of absence brought her, besides a cherished son? And, most important of all, how was he ever to expel this sorceress from his heart? With a vicious tug at the blind's cord Matt shut out these endless questions.

CHAPTER FIVE

In a grove known as Jacob's Acres the social event of the summer was underway. Strings of lights lit up the dark knoll; booths devoted to various handicrafts and games lined the neon perimeter. In the center iron cauldrons of hot grease crackled with catfish dipped in seasoned cornmeal. The succulent aroma tinged the warm night air. Spread upon picnic tables adorned with gaily checkered cloths were enormous bowls of coleslaw, platters of hush puppies, spicy condiments, and deep-dish blackberry cobbler. Ice-filled metal washtubs chilled bottles of cherry and orange soda pop for the children while, nearby, kegs of frothy beer and fermented cider appeased the grown-up palates.

Beneath a domed gazebo the county's best musicians were performing. The high-spirited twang of fiddles alternated with the Appalachian sound of dulcimers, the visceral appeal of the music worked its way with the crowd—feet tapped, whoops went up, and spirits soared. This midsummer's night festivity was a time of repletion —a time to escape troubles and strife, to simply enjoy the hills' freedom.

Matt weaved his way through a maze of swarming children, cider held high, a smile of remembrance upon his face. Their spontaneous glee and good-natured taunts recalled days gone by when he and Luke frolicked at the same event. The years had passed, the adolescent faces changed, yet the mood of frisky pups slipped off the leash still prevailed. The catfish fry meant no supervision, some stealthy sips of cider, and a late-night dare to jump the railroad ties until a locomotive's forlorn whistle and a rumbling in the tracks brought forth Farrett's Corners' newest hero.

He paused to take a swig of cider from his tin cup and nostalgically recall the past. There were times such as this one when yesteryear seemed like only yesterday. He found it hard to accept the present—a present that Luke no longer shared and one in which he often felt inadequate. His blue eyes grew hazy as his thoughts returned to another summer catfish fry and Luke's excited voice. His brother had sauntered up to him, hands in pockets, a mysterious grin upon his handsome face. . . .

"Bet you can't guess where I've been!" Luke teased.

"No, but I figure you're just bustin' to tell me." Matt tediously crunched a caramel apple, pretending nonchalance.

Luke flopped beside him on the picnic bench, linking his hands behind his head and staring up at the crescent moon. "I been killin' time at the sweets booth."

"Find anything you like?" Matt's white teeth worked a neat circle around the chewy surface as he mumbled the appropriate responses.

"Yeah, kinda. Blair Logan's serving. You know, she's grown up prettier and smarter than any other girl in this county."

Matt suddenly lost his taste for caramel. He threw the half-eaten remains into the brush with a vicious gesture. "Hadn't noticed," he scoffed.

"Well, I have. Somehow it doesn't seem quite fair that folks won't give her a chance just because she hails from the Hollow." Luke's face grew as earnestly pensive as his years would allow.

Matt abruptly stood up, wiping his sticky hands on the back of his pants and presenting his back to Luke. "Well, I guess it's like Pop says, 'People come in strata much like ore. It's not the way of things that they're mixed.' "

"Hooey! You're spoutin' Pop's hooey! You're sounding more and more like the old man every day." Luke rose up from his slouch to a defensive stance.

"And you're beginning to mimic Mama. If it wasn't for taking over the mines, I bet you'd end up some bleeding-heart politician."

All traces of light-heartedness left Luke's voice as he responded to Matt's prediction. "I'm not taking over the mines. Not now, now ever, Matt . . . ."

His brother's words, *"Not now . . . not ever,"* rang in Matt's ears as his vision cleared and he discovered himself back in the present, heir apparent to a dynasty. At that very moment, as he drank urgently from his tin cup once more, Blair's haunting profile appeared before him not ten feet away. Dressed in demure white, her auburn hair pulled high and adorned with pert daisies, she looked as fresh and fragile as a wood nymph. Unlike Matt and Luke, Blair had triumphed over the years—the hill's wayward daughter, at long last returned. But as Matt's view broadened to take in the reaction of the crowd, he knew her homecoming had only served to stir idle tongues and fire vivid imaginations.

His perceptive gaze noted the indignant glances, conspiratorial whispers, and purposely turned backs. His eyes

84

fell upon Danny at his mother's side. Dressed in crisply starched denims, a stylish Izod shirt, and snowy tennis shoes, he drew the curious attention of the other children. Smirking boys elbowed one another in the ribs and silly giggles spread among the girls. Matt watched sympathetically as Danny purposely smudged the bleached top of one shoe with the sole of the other. Uncomfortably he fidgeted beneath the gawking stares as his mother engaged Jim Akins in conversation. Though Matt believed children weren't born prejudiced, he felt they were endowed with a natural capacity for cruelty. He wondered how Blair, of all people, could have forgotten.

A snatch of conversation between Marybeth Simmons and Rachel Prentiss drifted his way as they sashayed by. So engrossed were they in vindictive speculation, Matt's presence nearby went undetected.

"Well," Marybeth crooned. "Ain't no one ever going to convince me that child of hers is a legitimate Hayden. Knowin' Blair Logan, he's probably just another scattered seed of a travelin' salesman."

"For sure," Rachel concurred. "I heard she worked for a spell as a waitress at that shabby truck-stop on the outskirts of Cooper's Town. Lord knows the riffraff that must've sampled her. I'll wager that boy is more heir to a diesel rig than any oil fortune."

The anger that uncoiled within Matt reinforced his feelings of protectiveness toward Danny. Regardless of Blair's refusal to concede Danny's true paternity, her bold counterattack and his own intuition left no doubt in Matt's mind. He *was* a Farrett! And no person, no town, would openly ridicule a Farrett in his presence. In this frame of mind Matt decided to keep a low profile and follow the ostracized Haydens around the festivities.

Jim Akins tucked Blair's fingertips in the crook of his arm and began a casual stroll toward the refreshment tables. He tried his best to be witty and diverting, hoping to compensate for the town's obvious coldness. In all his years as a clergyman he'd never before witnessed such unchristian, uncharitable behavior. Blair's smiles were rebuffed, her overtures ignored. Even Danny's impish charm had been met with universal resistance and little charity.

As he chatted and doted on Blair, his own heart absorbed her pain. She was trying to be brave, to pretend for his sake that the ongoing fiasco wasn't happening. But they both knew differently. Secretly they each comprehended that it was only out of respect for his position, not the goodness within their fellow man, that precluded a confrontation. If he lived out the rest of his days in this clannish community, he would never fully understand these people. They lived their lives by a dual standard—the Good Book and a hill code. And when one conflicted with the other, they conveniently abridged the Gospel to substantiate their harsh Ozark edict. But it was not his place to judge, merely guide. And deep in his soul Jim Akins remained firmly committed to the salvation of his flock. After what seemed like miles of unfriendly territory, he at last seated Blair and Danny at a picnic table and hurried to secure them a platter of delectable catfish.

A short distance away Matt idled by the cider keg and kept vigil. He, too, had observed the cold reception bestowed upon Blair and Danny. But unlike Rev Akins, Matt harbored no misconceptions about the climate of the town. Though he'd grown up with these people, called them neighbor, he remained leery of their peculiarities. He'd seen times when fairness or reason had nothing to do with their reactions. He admitted the hill creed's existence; moreover, he realized the depth of the townspeople's adherence to it.

He watched as Blair playfully ruffled her son's hair and pulled him close in a spontaneous hug. When she smiled at the boy, there shone a golden warmth in her eyes that dispelled Matt's uncertainty. During that silent exchange between mother and son it became abundantly clear to him that Blair loved Danny beyond reason. He suspected the child was the nucleus of her life. Now that he was privy to this secret, Matt came to fully realize the extent of Blair's maternal devotion. Hard, calculating Blair Logan was actually capable of selfless love. A pang of regret coursed through him as he noted the tender way in which her fingertips smoothed the boy's hair. Years ago, if they'd been more trusting, fate kinder, it might have been his son, rather than his nephew, whom she now protected and adored.

After Rev Akins's return, as he observed the threesome's intimate byplay as they ate, Matt's mood altered. He found himself tightening at the fond glances exchanged by Jim and Blair; discovered himself resenting the beaming regard on Danny's freckled face. Jim Akins was a good man, his morals only of the purest, his intellect of the highest. But Matt silently denounced his association with Blair. They were of different worlds, he and Blair— she a realist, he an idealist. He could never completely understand her life, nor she fully enter his. This Matt knew and unconsciously counted upon.

His tummy full and growing restless with grown-up banter, Danny begged his mother's permission to wander around the game booths. Blair shot Jim an apprehensive look, but he quickly masked their concern with a flip of a silver dollar and his blanket permission. "Don't spend it all in one place."

"Gonna try my luck at the BB shoot!" Danny exclaimed, darting into the maze of shuffling people. Neither Danny, Jim, or Blair were cognizant of Matt's persistent surveillance.

The BB shoot being the most popular of booths, Danny had to wriggle his way in close. He stood for a curious moment, his small hand anxiously fingering the silver dollar burning like molten lead within his pocket. This was *real* he-man stuff—a test of marksmanship and merit. Danny's exuberance overrode his inexperience. A space cleared at the counter. Before Danny had thought better on it, he moseyed up and slammed his silver dollar down.

"Well, looky here, boys. We got us a city slicker who wants to show us what fer," the craggy woodsy behind the counter bellowed. "Say, boy, you even know which end to point?" The onlookers burst into laughter at the old codger's joshing.

"Yes, sir." Danny's polite reply was interpreted as intimidation. A wiry Crawford boy, attired in only bibbed overalls and a pair of dilapidated sandals, stepped forth from the crowd.

"Hey, now, ain't he polite 'n' all. I say, a fancy-breeches fella like him ought not to be sassed, old man. Give him a gun and a load, and let's have a look-see what the city boy can do." Though the scraggly Crawfords weren't too terribly popular around town, this once the eldest, Jeremiah, drew unanimous support. Bad, ugly, and near-illit-erate, at least, he was one of their own.

Matt clenched his teeth to impose restraint. He knew by Danny's sizing inspection of Jeremiah that he sensed the implication of the challenge. A feeling of helplessness, and extreme pride, encompassed Matt as he watched the drama unfold. The bearded woodsy inside the booth laid a rifle and ammunition before Danny, spat a brown stream of tobacco at his feet, and said, "You got two practice shots afore taking three in earnest. That'll be two bits." Danny silently slid his silver dollar over to the woodsy before testing the foreign feel of the gun.

"Tell ya what, city boy," Jeremiah sneered. "I gotta dollar against your change that says I kin beat your best shot out of three with jest one. Lessen you're ascared, of course?"

Matt gulped his cider in lieu of speaking up. It was then that he noticed Blair and Rev Akins standing nearby and exercising the same self-discipline. He observed the pale tension which gripped Blair's face at her son's impetuous "You're on!" Jim Akins's supportive grip on her elbow tried to alleviate the strain. They all three knew that Danny didn't completely comprehend the undercurrents filtering through the rancorous crowd. There was much more at stake than a mere silver dollar.

Matt could tell by the awkward way that Danny han-dled the rifle that he'd had little experience. He wasn't the only one. Jeremiah looked over his shoulder to shoot a wicked wink at his brothers. The city slicker was about to get slicked! Danny mimed the Westerns he'd absorbed on TV, held the rifle loosely against his shoulder, took a bead, and shot at the moving metal target. The BB hit far to the left with a ineffectual *ping*. Matt and Blair watched helplessly on as their son hurried another frustrating practice shot and missed once more.

The Crawford bully cackled aloud. "Done used up your practice shots, city boy. Sure am gonna enjoy takin' your highfalutin mama's money."

Danny lurched for Jeremiah, but Matt was quicker. With a restraining hand upon the boy's shoulder he whispered a warning in his ear. "He's trying to rile you, boy. Lose your temper now, and he'll win more than a dollar." When the startled boy turned to stare up at his coach, the Farrett chin squared and he nodded reluctantly. A murmur went through the onlookers as Matt's hand remained clamped on the boy's shoulder and he offered instruction in a low, soothing voice. "Hold the butt firm against your shoulder, sight in with your right eye, and ease the trigger back slowly."

The sight of Matt standing beside Danny, his bulk shielding him from malevolent stares, nearly caused Blair's knees to buckle. The strain of the past few moments had taken their toll. She could withstand the town's cruelty herself, but not when it was directed toward her son. She'd never been more grateful or beholden in her life. Jim Akins's arm moved to her waist. He knew she was totally unaware of the weak slump of her body against his bracing weight.

Danny followed Matt's instructions, pulling the butt of the rifle tight, aiming carefully, and squeezing the trigger easily. The first of his three shots hit right of center. Matt pressed his fingers reassuringly upon his arm. Danny relaxed and tried again. The shot rang close, but slightly high. Standing apart from the crowd, Blair closed her eyes and prayed for divine intervention. She knew Jim Akins would think her request petty, but then he hadn't endured the hills as long as she.

One more word of advice, then Matt patted Danny's back and gave him space. "Take a deep breath, hold it, and shoot." Danny did exactly as instructed. His breath held, his arm steady, he aimed and fired. The BB hit dead center! Danny relaxed, laying the rifle upon the counter and psyching his opponent with a murderous glare.

Jeremiah wiped his sweaty palms on the back of his overalls and stepped up. Like Sergeant York, he wetted down his sights with a fingertip, lazily drew a bead, and squeezed the trigger. The BB pinged only centimeters from the bull's-eye; a good shot, *but not good enough!*

Disappointed mumbles circulated through the crowd, but then Matt's commanding voice regained everyone's undivided attention. "I think there's a small matter of a silver dollar, Jeremiah . . ." Matt's steel-blue eyes immobilized the bully.

Jeremiah tossed his unruly hair defiantly and crawfished. "I ain't got it on me right now."

"Danny will take your promise to leave it with Rev Akins. He knows that a hill boy wouldn't make a wager he couldn't own up to." Matt quirked a brow, calling the cocky Jeremiah's bluff.

"Yes, sir" came the sullen response as the crowd parted for Matt and Danny's march back to Blair.

Danny had never been so excited, but he managed to curb the impulse to make an elated dash for his mother and keep the manly pace beside his champion. Somehow Blair found the strength to retain her own composure. The wild racing of her heart could be attributed to more than just Danny's victory. As the two most special men in her life reached her side, only a broad, pleased smile gave Blair away.

"I'm so proud of you, Danny," she beamed.

"I couldn't have done it without . . ." Danny hesitated, turning to gaze dumbfoundedly up at the tall man beside him. "I don't even know your name, mister."

"Matt," Blair half-whispered, her grateful eyes meeting and holding the crystal gaze which had spanned miles and years. Then getting a grip on herself, she cleared her throat and completed the introduction. "This is Matthew Farrett, Danny."

A small hand extended in a large gesture. "Thanks, Matt." Danny's coloring might be his mother's, but the winning smile, the determined chin, belonged exclusively to the Farretts.

Matt's hand encased the boy's. He held tight and long to the flesh and blood he cherished. "You're welcome, Danny. A few more lessons and you'll be a bona fide marksman."

"Would you teach me, Matt?" Danny blurted out.

Blair rushed to intercede. "You shouldn't impose, Danny. Matt's a busy man." She placed a guarding hand on her son's shoulder.

Matt smiled at her obviousness. "I'm not *that* busy, and Danny is anything but an imposition." He directed his approving gaze to Danny. "Noon, day after tomorrow at Farrett House."

"You betcha, Matt," Danny whooped, totally oblivious to his mother's reprimanding scowl.

"Then, I'll be saying goodnight." Matt ruffed the boy's

hair, adding a cordial "Blair . . . Rev Akins . . ." before moving on.

"He's a pretty swell guy, Mom. He a friend of yours?" Danny's candid question jolted Blair out of a pensive stare. Noting her startled speechlessness, Jim came to her rescue.

"Well, he's certainly your pal. I tell you, all this excitement has worked up my thirst. How about I treat us to cool drink?"

"A cup of cider?" Danny pressed his luck.

"Cherry pop," the reverend qualified, casting Blair a conspiratorial wink as he took her arm.

Shortly after the promised drinks and one more leisurely stroll about the grounds, Blair insisted upon Danny's curfew. Being a gentleman of the old school, nothing would do Reverend Akins but to see them home. After tucking Danny in and praising his feat one last time, Blair joined Jim on the back porch. He sat perched upon the wooden railing, gazing up at the moon.

"It'll rain tomorrow," he predicted, sensing rather than hearing her approach.

She half-sat on the rail and leaned her back against the cedar post. "Now, how do you know that?" Her voice held a hint of mirth.

"The signs are there—a haze around the moon, no stars in the sky. Signs are always evident to those who want to read them." He turned to face her, a furrow of concern creasing his forehead. "What unforgivable sin do these people think you guilty of?"

Unaccustomed to anything but lightheartedness from Jim, Blair had no immediate comeback. She sighed, looked up at the starless sky, and collected her thoughts.

"Mostly my rebelliousness. I think in me they see a side of themselves they'd prefer not to admit—discontentment, impatience, yearning. There's a fierce pride that exists in these hills—you don't challenge life; you endure it. I never learned to abide restrictions, and for this I'm labeled a rebel."

She never even noticed Jim's lithe descent to the ground until his strong hands clamped about her waist and he lifted her to the damp grass. Her hazel eyes opened wide at the gentle pressure of his fingertips. "I see and hear only human qualities in you, Blair, certainly nothing for which you need repent. You're a special lady with a rare and wondrous capacity for life." He tipped her chin with a fingertip to delicately place a kiss on her unsuspecting lips. Then, smiling at her awed expression, he tweaked her upturned nose as he took his leave. "These things about you are as certain as tomorrow's rain. I read signs." His parting words mingled with the darkness.

Crouched and careful, Blair made her way down the steep grade and over rocky boulders to the edge of Beaver's Creek. She banged her shin against a jutting outcrop and grimaced in pain. Easing herself onto a flat boulder, she rubbed the bruised area with her palm and fought back a sudden urge to cry. It wasn't the bruised flesh that hurt so much; it was her tormented mind. This night had wrought more than she could contend with—the town's blatant rebuff, Danny's near calamity, Matt's unexpected intervention, and Jim's loyal declaration. At the moment it was the latter that bothered her most. Why else would she have struck out for Beaver's Creek?

This rugged terrain was more than just a dot left off a

tour map; it was her and Luke Farrett's secret place. Here they often met to enjoy long and probing discussions, to share private joys and sorrows, seek shelter and find a friend. How many years ago was it? Her mind rippled to the tune of the creek. Now it seemed impossible that she and Luke had ever been that young or innocent. She knew that it was the similarity between kind and gentle Jim Akins and Luke Farrett that had triggered the need to revisit this mournful spot. She hadn't been back here since that night long ago when she and Luke were to have their final and most honest talk.

Luke had always been so gracious to her. It was *his* outstretched hand that pulled her up from town's pettiness; *his* easy, magnetic smile that made everything else seem inconsequential in comparison. He was her one true friend in all the world—her confidant, her refuge. And theirs was a mutual need. To her he would tell his dreams, admit his fears; with her he could be himself, not what his family expected of him. Here at Beaver's Creek they laughed and commiserated, debated and resolved. And here they said their good-byes, not suspecting that their farewells would be forever.

Blair's fingertips dabbled in the cool creek waters. It seemed the only reality in a haze of besieging memories. Her eyes clouded as she recalled the last, bittersweet meeting between her and Luke. That night when she joined Luke on the moss-covered rocks, her young heart carried a burden far beyond her years. Two hours earlier she'd been informed by Doc Sercy of her confirmed pregnancy. She was six weeks with child—Matt's child. In all their many discussions, whether by accident or design, she and Luke never mentioned Matt. Thinking back on it now,

Blair wondered if she'd intuitively guessed Luke's unde-
clared feelings, yet, in her naiveté, chose to interpret them
in the only way she could bear to.

After one glance of her strained features Luke offered
his hand, guided her dazed steps to their favorite rock, and
then huddled close in silence. He patiently waited for the
explanation he knew she would eventually offer.

"I'm pregnant, Luke." The declaration came numbly.
His strong arm wrapped comfortingly about her trembling
shoulders.

"Will the father marry you?" he asked softly.

"I haven't told him." A shudder ran through her slender frame, and Luke pulled her nearer to stave off her
despair.

"Is there any reason other than pride that holds your
tongue?"

"Yes," she rasped. "Knowing your brother, Luke, do
you think he'd ever believe me anything other than a
conniving opportunist out to entrap him?" She'd confessed the worst and stated the obvious all in one breath.
Luke stiffened beside her. For a breathless moment she
feared he'd forsake her like everyone else. But then his
hand cupped her cheek and guided her defeated gaze to
his sympathetic blue-green eyes. For the very first time she
saw in them the words he'd never spoken. He loved her
. . . good, bad, or indifferent, Luke Farrett truly loved
Blair Logan.

"Do you honestly believe in your heart that he doesn't
care? That he wouldn't understand or live up to his obligation?"

Blair broke free from his probing gaze, staring down at
the babbling creek. Somehow the endless stream reminded

96

her of their lives—a predestined course, swift and unalter-able. "He cared once, briefly. I don't want his understand-ing or obligation. I want to be loved." She choked on the futility of her hopes, unwilled tears trickling down her cheeks.

Luke hugged her close, brushing her auburn hair with soft, consoling strokes. "It's been said that no one knows a man as thoroughly as a woman. I only know my brother in a limited way—as one man knows another. If you're sure Matt offers no solution, then take mine."

Blair rocked her head miserably against his shoulder. "What is it you think I should do, Luke?"

"Marry me," he stated flatly.

With a startled lurch, Blair straightened up, her con-fused eyes boring deep into his heart. He read the mistak-en assumption in her eyes.

"It's not pity, Blair. I may not love you in the fiery way Matt does, but I do care." He noted her unconscious withdrawal. Grasping her shoulders firmly, his fingers squeezed to emphasize the one practical point he had to drive home. "The baby needs a father, and I'm offering you the chance to give the child its rightful name. Don't think of me as self-sacrificing, Blair. In fact, for my own selfish reasons, it's me who's clinging to you."

"Oh, Luke!" she cried, throwing her arms about him and burying her head against his chest. "I'm tempted, believe me I am. You're a sensitive, wonderful man, but . . ."

"But . . ." His lips, buried deep within her fragrant hair, completed her rejection. ". . . you'll always love my broth-er more."

She nodded mutely.

"I understand," he lied.

His dejected tone inspired her further explanation. "No, you don't, Luke, not really." She forced her heartsick body upright and captured his pained face between palms. "I'm caught between the two of you. One I've loved since I was small—fiercely and passionately, with the other, I've only just recently discovered his tenderness and sincerity. Matt came first and caught me, but you, Luke, were like a godsend. I can't deny you a chance at complete happiness. You deserve much more than to live in your brother's shadow. Please, understand why I have to refuse." Her haunted eyes searched his face as she held her breath and awaited his reply.

"Sometimes I think I understand you better than you do yourself." His hands grasped hers and held them tightly. "What will you do, Blair?"

"Leave Farrett's Corner tonight. I don't know exactly where I'm going, but anywhere away from here has got to be better. I can't subject this child to the ridicule of this town."

He didn't argue. Instead he fumbled in his pocket and pressed money into her shaking hand. "Take it!" He squelched her arguments before she could voice them. "My niece or nephew needs a start."

"Dear Luke, I do love you," she moaned, collapsing against the solidness of him.

They embraced. They cried. They parted.

Ten years later sitting beside a creek whose swift and impetuous current reminded her of their runaway lives, Blair Hayden sobbed once more. The sound was wretched, her pain even greater.

CHAPTER SIX

"You don't think he's forgotten, do you, Mom? Maybe we should've called first? What if—?"

"Danny, please!" Blair's own nervousness sharpened her tone. Immediately a wave of guilt washed over her at her son's wounded look. Ever since she had gotten up this morning his excitement had heightened along with her moody impatience. Over breakfast he'd once more expounded to Grams the tale of the great BB match. Not only did he add sound effects to the nth degree, but the whole episode was beginning to take on the dimensions of another Gunfight at the O.K. Corral, with him and Matt starring as the legendary Wyatt Earp and Doc Holliday.

Blair weaved the Ferrari around the last curve leading to Farrett House. Once, turning onto the gravel access road, she impulsively reached over and squeezed Danny's hand.

"I'm sorry I snapped. I'm certain Matt hasn't forgotten. He's probably every bit as anxious to see you as you are to see him."

A broad, forgiving smile broke across the tiny freckled face. Then, as his watchful eyes left his mother to stare ahead, a disbelieving whistle passed his lips. "Holy Moses! Would you look at that!" Having been accustomed to wealth all of his young life, Blair knew that it was the stateliness of Farrett House that impressed her son. The late-nineteenth-century structure, looming at the crest of the mountain, dominated the clovered highland. This was by no means a small feat, since the countryside itself, with its aloof pines and mist-blue bluffs, vied for supremacy. Remembering her own feelings of awe the first time she'd ever laid eyes on Farrett House, Blair smiled to herself at Danny's agape expression.

They cleared the main gates and drove the steep grade to the semicircular driveway out front. No sooner had Blair shifted into park when Matt's familiar figure stepped out onto the primrose-covered veranda.

"Hey ya, Matt!" Danny waved as he all but tore the door off the hinges trying to get out.

"You'll get out a lot quicker if you unlock the door," Blair sighed, leaning over to provide assistance. No sooner had the lock clicked than Danny sprung from the car like a jack rabbit, leaving his mother stretched across the seat and groping for the door handle. Only when her downcast eyes caught sight of a pair of snakeskin boots did Blair realize Matt's nearness. But before she could boost herself upright, he leaned inside the opened door frame with a casual "Hello, Blair."

As she struggled to get up, the strap of her middy blouse slipped off one ivory shoulder. Matt's eyes did not miss the split-second view of her braless state. He remained motionless, caught in an unexpected backwash of memories.

"Howdy, Matt," Blair drawled, slipping back into familiar dialect to cover her uneasiness. A slight grin tugged at the corners of his mouth, as if he saw through her smokescreen. Quickly she hastened his departure. "You can reach me at the farm when target practice is over. If Danny misbehaves, don't hesitate to call sooner."

"I've been thinking, Blair," he stalled. "Instead of making two trips, why don't you just wait here. After Danny and I have our shooting session, we could have lunch and then ride over the grounds."

Total shock registered upon Blair's sensitive face. After all that had happened between them lately, a luncheon invitation was the last thing she expected from Matt Farrett. As much as she appreciated his intervention on Danny's behalf a few days ago, she also recalled his prior threat—"Tomorrow will be looking over your shoulder." Her apprehensive thoughts were reflected in her voice.

"I thank you, Matt, but I have some errands that need tendin' to." Under his intense scrutiny her fingers fidgeted with the single braid cascading over her shoulder.

"Awww, Mom!" Danny's cherub face poked from under Matt's arm. "You can do those old errands anytime. Matt and I want you to stay. Don't we, Matt?" His upturned hazel eyes prompted a reiteration of the offer. With unaccustomed lightheartedness Matt locked Danny's neck in a playful bearhug as he shot Blair a reassuring wink.

"It'll be a nice afternoon, Blair. I promise."

The words were direct and simple; the implication behind them anything but. Could it be that for one glorious day they would declare a truce? Enjoy the sunshine's warmth, the air's purity, and the joy of the child that bound them? The peaceful promise superseded caution. With a meaningful gesture, Blair removed the keys from the ignition, dropped them in her purse, and got out of the car.

"Gentlemen," she laughed. "I'll await you on the veranda." Blair pretended not to notice the smug looks they exchanged as she ran gingerly up the steps and flopped into the porch swing. "Well, do you mean to just stand there all day?" she goaded, sending them scurrying for the Cherokee.

Watching the chattering Danny scuffle up to his prestigious shotgun position, Blair smiled to herself. Though Danny had always been a happy child, she couldn't recall another time when he'd been quite so ecstatic. It was as if, without his knowing why, he instinctively knew he was treading upon ancestral ground—where he belonged, where he'd *always* belonged. With a departing honk the Cherokee hauled down the road.

"You got some special place in mind, Matt?" Danny mimicked his champion's posture, angling his body and hanging an elbow out the window.

Matt glanced in his direction at the question, smiled, and then returned his eyes to the road.

"I do, in fact, Danny. My brother and I used to take target practice at the very spot."

"That's probably how you got so good, huh?"

"I don't know about good, but I can hold my own. You know, Danny, being capable with a gun isn't something you show off with. True marksmen don't flaunt their skill or ever abuse it. Do you understand what I'm telling you?"

"Sure, Matt. You mean not to bully like Jeremiah Crawford, or use a gun to do wrong."

"Couldn't have put it better myself." Matt grinned, guiding the Cherokee off the road and through high grass to a secluded gully's edge. Typically Danny jumped from the jeep just as the wheels ground to a halt.

"Man! This is a terrific spot. Why, even the targets are still standing across the gully."

"They're new ones, Danny. I set them up yesterday." Matt cleared the jeep and sauntered to the rear to get the rifles. "Come over here and pick which one you want."

In bounding leaps Danny cleared the distance, his eyes sparkling with admiration as he spied the rifles Matt held. Their blued barrels shone in the bright sunlight and the hand-etched wooden stocks gleamed like precious teak. Danny didn't know much about firearms, but he knew quality when he saw it. Lovingly his small hand traced each polished stock until, at last, he chose the Remington over the Winchester. He'd chosen Luke's rifle—the one stored in the gun cabinet for years. Matt had refurbished and tested it yesterday. A knot formed in his throat as he saw Danny take it in his small hands, then bring it up to sight it with Luke's familiar mannerisms.

"That one belonged to my brother," Matt heard himself say.

"Don't he use it anymore?" Danny asked innocently.

Matt felt his heart constrict. "No," he replied dazedly. "Not anymore."

Danny lowered the rifle to stare up at him with curious eyes. Matt seemed preoccupied, his gaze drifting across the gully in search of something Danny could not distinguish. Wanting his hero's undivided attention, Danny tugged on his shirtsleeve. "Can't we get started now, Matt?"

Matt looked down at the boy. With a vivid portrait of his brother fresh in his mind he saw similarities, but then, for a brief instant, he thought he perceived something more—something undefined and disturbing—something

103

that defied explanation and only registered in the heart. Becoming aware of Danny's concerned look, Matt forced himself to withdraw from these thoughts and feelings he could not interpret. Ruffling the boy's copper hair, he reassured him with a weak smile and a challenge. "If you're waiting on me, you're backing up!"

"Okay!" Danny whooped, romping across the high grass and shouting a million questions back over his shoulder.

Matt stood rooted, some nagging intuition weighting him to the spot. What or why he did not know. It was like the light of dawn, hovering beyond the horizon, but not yet fully broken.

The porch swing creaked to an idle rhythm. Lethargically Blair rocked back and forth, back and forth. Just like the swinging motion, her emotions oscillated wildly, to and fro, to and fro.

Beware! her mind cautioned. Matt doesn't forgive or forget. Be fair! her heart pleaded. Danny is his son.

Blair's hand grasped the metal chain tightly—so tightly that the links marked her palm. Slowly she unclenched her fist, examining the indented pattern upon her flesh—the interacting design. This was the way their lives were linked—she and Matt shackled with guilt, Danny and Luke caught up in a chain reaction. Blair stopped the rocking of the swing. She wished she could so easily halt the momentum of their lives.

Abruptly she stood up. Walking to the railing of the veranda, she reached out to touch a primrose. The texture felt velvety soft, pleasing and seductive. Yet nestled among this beauty lay the inevitable thorns. Matt was

104

composed of just such a mixture of splendor and hurt. Whatever the future held, she must never disregard the past. The distinctive whine of the Cherokee snapped her head up and put her on guard. A squeal of brakes and the slam of two doors produced a hyperactive boy and grinning chaperon before her.

"Matt's the best shot this side of the Mason-Dixon, Mom," Danny boasted. "But, I tell ya, a little more practice and I'm going to be better."

"And so modest too," Blair grinned, slipping her hands into her jean pockets and rolling her eyes heavenward at Matt. His returning smile caused shades of long ago to rush over her.

"How about lunch? You think you can handle that as well as a Remington?" Matt's arm lighted on Danny's shoulder. Together they set a spry pace toward Blair.

"Could I! I'm so hungry I could eat two desserts." Blair shook her head disapprovingly as she joined them.

"Well, we'll see if your mouth just wrote a check you're stomach can't cash," Matt teased, leading his guests through the front foyer and into the dining room.

"Wow! This place is super neat, Matt. You live here all by yourself?" Danny plopped into a high-backed Victorian chair and inspected the enormous crystal-prismed chandelier suspended overhead.

Matt exchanged uncomfortable glances with Blair before answering. "At the moment I do. My mother is convalescing at a hospital not far from here."

"What about your brother? You know, the one who doesn't use the Remington anymore. Doesn't he live here, too?"

Blair's face paled as she literally dropped into a chair.

This time Matt avoided her eyes as he explained in a voice totally devoid of emotion, "He hasn't lived here for quite some time, Danny. I'll tell cook we're ready to eat." And parting the paned french doors, he disappeared. Danny sat swinging his legs and scanning the portraits that were hung about the room. Blair rubbed her temples and closed her eyes against painful memories.

Upon Matt's return, a feast fit for a young boy was served. The entire menu had been planned as a ten-year-old's delight—burgers grilled to perfection, crispy golden french fries, tumblers of Coca-Cola, and still-warm cherry pie.

As Blair nibbled her food and watched her son absorb Matt's cuisine and conversation, an oppressive sense of guilt settled on her shoulders. Danny was totally enraptured with Matt. He hung on his every word, devoured him with his awestruck, trusting gaze. Added to her misery was the extra burden of Matt's devotion to Danny. It was obvious to her that he'd spent every free hour since the catfish fry planning for this visit. It also became painfully clear that their bloodtie had drawn them together. She'd witnessed the strong bond between Matt and Luke, and now the cycle was being repeated once more. Only this time the Farrett bond wasn't brother to brother, it was father to son.

Her fork toyed with the flaky piecrust, her mind with regret. How wonderful it would be if Luke had lived to share in this day. To know of his nephew's security and his brother's joy. Haunting "if onlys" reeled in Blair's mind. If only Matt knew he looked upon his son. If only her prideful silence could be broken, and she could make up for all the lost years with a word. But "if onlys" changed nothing, and the burden of silence was hers alone to bear.

"Isn't that true, Blair?" Matt's faraway voice reclaimed her.

"Ah, what? I'm sorry, I must've been daydreaming." Blair's dull eyes brightened with feigned interest.

Matt studied her for a moment, then repeated himself. "Isn't it true that a yell from Old Baldy echoes a good two miles?"

Blair nodded her agreement, then turned to gaze out the bay window at the legendary mountain beyond. Even past midday a vaporous mist clung to its summit—the gorged and barren peak that inspired the mountain's name deceptively hidden behind a gossamer cloud. Why did the sight remind her of her own cruel masquerade? And why couldn't she stop thinking in these terms?

The touch of Matt's hand upon her shoulder startled her. "Are you feeling all right?" he asked, his voice bland yet his touch extremely gentle.

"I'm fine," she lied, her eyes falling upon Danny's empty chair. "Where's he run off to now?" she sighed.

"He's waiting for us at the stables, anxious to begin the ride."

As she rose from her chair, Matt's hand slid from her shoulder down her bare arm. The mere graze of his flesh against hers still sent yearning bolts coursing through her body. She took a step backward to neutralize the effect.

"Then, I suppose we shouldn't delay. My instincts tell me that Danny won't be patient long." Without glancing in his direction, she walked silently beside him as they adjourned to the stables.

"Which one do I get to ride, Matt?" Danny jiggled from foot to foot, hardly able to contain himself.

"I thought Navajo would be more your style." Matt led the good-natured pinto pony from a forward stall and saddled him up. Once Danny was in the saddle, he begged Matt's permission to jaunt the corral until his mother and Matt had joined him.

Matt went about readying his Arabian, Desperado, and the high-spirited filly he'd appropriately named Fickle Lady. Only now and then did he cast a perplexed look in Blair's direction, but each time she veiled her expression or turned her head. Her peculiar sullenness bothered him. Like the spirited filly, Blair always radiated vitality. At times she channeled it into hidden courses, but always it was there. This was a side to her he'd never seen before. Her mood bordered on apathy, a condition he despised.

"All set," he prompted, pulling the cinch tight. "Fickle Lady is all yours."

Blair strode to the filly's side. For the first time today he detected a flash of golden spunk in her eyes. "I suppose you think Fickle Lady is *exactly* my style." She grabbed the horn and hoisted herself into the saddle without assistance.

"I think you're being especially sensitive." He shot her a goading grin before mounting Desperado. With a tilt of her head she nudged the platinum-maned filly forward.

"Join up, Danny," Matt hollered as he took the lead and trotted Desperado across the wide-open acreage. They followed the perimeter of the Farrett estate—three horses, three riders, three shadows in the midafternoon sun. Matt pointed out historical points of interest and unusual features of the land while giving a concise history of the Farretts' acquisition of the land. Danny was enthralled, but only for a half-hour or so. Before too long, he began to trot ahead, familiarizing himself with the terrain at a child's pace. Matt reined in Desperado, falling back and imposing his company upon the sulky Blair.

"Now, that we have a minute, I'd like to ask you some questions about Hayden Petroleum, Blair."

"Such as?" She kept her eyes focused on her son ahead.

"Such as, how is it that you acted alone when you acquired our note? I would think that you'd be accountable to a board of directors, and securing backing for such a major undertaking would've taken time—time you didn't waste."

"I own seventy-five percent of Hayden Petroleum's stock. I don't necessarily need the board's approval before acting."

"How nice to inherit such power." Now Matt was staring straight ahead, his jaw tightening in a gesture she knew so well.

"I only inherited fifty-one percent. I had to fight like hell to keep what I had and acquire the remaining shares. While I was married to Jess Hayden, my only contact with power was entertaining it—a duty I owed and performed very well. As his widow, I was expected to bow out gracefully and not concern myself with matters I was incapable of handling." A bitter note crept into her voice. "Jess shocked his family, the board, practically everyone in Dallas by leaving a controlling share in his company to me. At first they thought me naive enough to relinquish his bequest. Then they thought I was an imbecile who'd accept their gracious offer of a figurehead chairmanship in return for the forfeiture of half my shares."

Matt noted her grip on the reins—fast and cleaving. He knew the outcome of her story before she told it. After all, who better than he should realize the grit of Blair Logan?

"It was quite a scene, Matt—the widow in mourning black telling them all to go straight to hell. Jess had his reasons for leaving the bulk of his holdings in my hands. He'd spent days, months, and years grooming me to carry on in his stead. And I had my reasons for complying—to see that my late husband's wishes were carried out and insure my son's inheritance."

Her hands relaxed upon the leather. Matt could almost feel the tension leave her body. "I was a diligent student. But even though I'm capable, I have to fight every day of my life to fend the jackals off. Greed's an insatiable hunger. It feeds on the weak. I learned the hard way never to be that—weak. I have few friends, even fewer associates I trust, but no one preys on me or mine."

The woman riding at his side was a revelation. Her tale surpassed anything that Matt had suspected. No longer did he view her as the beautiful enchantress Blair Logan. He now realized she'd earned the name Hayden. She was intelligent, gutsy, and confident. Besides which, she was also a mother fighting for the survival of her young. There seemed to be very little he could fault her for. He reached over and reined in Fickle Lady at Desperado's side. For a suspended moment, as the animals flicked and flinched, their riders sat in reflective silence.

"You're a strange and strong woman, Blair Hayden." Matt gazed at her long and evaluatingly.

Afraid he would read the emptiness in her eyes, Blair glanced away. The hunger she felt shed out upon the distant mountains. They appeared like smoky mirages when viewed through a shimmer of heat. "I've usually found the word *strange* is often applied to that which is misunderstood."

"An interesting interpretation, Mrs. Hayden. Perhaps you have a point."

Blair turned to him, capturing a moment and a look she'd forgotten existed—true tenderness.

CHAPTER SEVEN

"I'm still not sure this is such a good idea." Lurlene
Hershell lagged behind as Marybeth Simmons proceeded
through Grams Logan's gate and into the yard.

"Will you quit your whining and get on in here."
Marybeth drew up with a disgusted sigh. She balanced the
tin of homemade pralines on the palm of one hand and
touched her tightly bound chignon with the other. Sheepishly her co-conspirator joined her. Standing side by side,
they looked like Siamese twins in their starched gingham
housedresses and dime-store accessories.

"I don't know, Marybeth." Lurlene's bulging eyes
scanned the deserted yard. "Something deep in my bones
says Blair Logan ain't gonna take kindly to our droppin'
in unannounced. Besides, what do you figure to learn? It
ain't like she's gonna confide in us."

"I told you, I just want to get a good look at the boy.
Ain't likely she's gonna turn us away. Not with me toting
my special pralines as a present to the youngun."
Marybeth's free hand still primped. Now it moved to the
torturous girdle binding her engorged hips.

"Aren't you ever gonna give up suspectin' that boy's the
seed of one of our men? I'm tellin' you, Marybeth, you'd
best let sleepin' dogs lie. You're fixin' to stir up a hornet's
nest for sure. Remember how fired up Rachel got when
you blurted out that Lloyd used to be Blair's steady at the

112

Dixie Belle luncheon?" Lurlene shook her head at the dismal recollection.

"She overreacts to everything. A case of the nerves, if you ask me. All I said was that Lloyd used to date the boy's mother; I never declared him the father. And you can quit acting so damn lily-white pure. The only reason your precious Hershell ain't suspect is cause he had the good fortune not to move here until after Blair skipped town. The rest of us got plenty to be suspicious about. Now, go on up there and knock on the door."

"Me!" Lurlene wailed. "Listen here, bossy, it's you who's so bent on socializin'. I'll hold the pralines, and you do your own knockin'." Stubbornly Lurlene held out her hand.

With a scathing look Marybeth slammed the tin into her palm. "You always was a lily-liver, Lurlene—shaking and quakin' at everythin'. You drop those, and I'll cut your heart out."

At the threat the cowardly Lurlene clutched the tin tight against her meager bosom. Meanwhile Marybeth tugged at her housedress, squared her double chin, and began to march toward the back porch. Her Red-Cross pumps had only paced off a few feet when the back door swung open and Blair stepped out onto the porch with a shotgun beneath her arm. Warily Marybeth drew up.

"Can I do something for you, Marybeth?" The civility in Blair's voice belied the hard glint in her eyes.

"'Lo, Blair. Me and Lurlene thought it'd be neighborly to drop by and pay a social call." Nervously Marybeth substantiated Lurlene's trembling presence with a backward flip of her hand.

"How nice, seein' as how in all the years we've known each other you've never been social before."

"Well, no time like the present, that's what I always say." Marybeth's mouth quivered slightly as she forced a flimsy smile. "I brought some of my special recipe pralines for your boy. If he's around I'd—"

"He's not," Blair snapped. "So, you might as well take your pralines and get."

"Well, I never!" Marybeth huffed, her spine stiffening at the insult.

"You got that right. You never committed a kind act in your life that didn't harbor some sneaky motive." Blair raised the shotgun meaningfully. "I don't have to be a mind reader to know the both of you are up to no good. You got the look of a couple of weasels skulking around a chicken coop. Now, get off my grandmother's property before I show you what you can do with those pralines."

Retreat seemed the only prudent action when looking down the barrel of a thirty-ought-six. Marybeth nearly fell over the petrified Lurlene as she backed away. With a brusque shove against the latter's shoulder she scurried them toward the gate like two ruffled, clucking hens. But as Marybeth fumbled with the latch, she dared to have the last word before marking good her escape. "Pure bitch, that's what you are, Blair Logan!" she screeched.

Blair cocked the shotgun and fired a round up into the air, sending the tin of pralines and petticoats flying. "I would've thought that fact was established years ago!" she hollered after them a smile of satisfaction fleeting across her sultry lips.

The last Blair heard from the two busybodies was Marybeth's shrill warning above a furious bang of car

114

doors. "Say a word about this, and I'll cut your tongue out. I swear it, Lurlene!"

"Oh, shut up and drive!" came the disgusted reply.

Throughout the rest of the day, and even into the twilight hours, a triumphant smirk lingered on Blair's face. Every time she thought back on the scene a feeling of total gratification filled her. For years she'd longed for a taste of revenge, and today she had feasted.

"Feelin' mighty pleased with yourself, ain't ya?" Grams stepped out of the screen door, wiped her hands on the tail of her apron, then leveled a disapproving look at her granddaughter.

At her reproachful tone Blair's wily grin faded. "Some," she admitted, fixing her eyes on Danny as he chased lightning bugs with a mason jar across the yard.

"Some! Hmmph! I suppose about the only thing that'd make you feel better is blowin' 'em clean in two. You got a mean streak in you, gal." Grams arched a brow, always a sure sign of an impending lecture.

"And I suppose you'd have preferred for me to be more hospitable while they connive to hurt my son." Seldom did Blair talk to her grandmother in such a manner. No sooner had she spoken the words than she regretted them.

The old woman drew herself up, her keen eyes stern, her voice sharp. "Don't sass me, gal. And don't try to pull the wool over my eyes, neither. What you did this afternoon was as much for yourself as for Danny. You been storin' up pain and grudgin' till you're about to burst. Oh, I know it's been said that revenge is sweet, but I say it's sour. 'N' iffen you aren't careful, it'll fester and spread till it consumes the good and leave only a rotten core. I've spoke my piece. Now think on it." With those weighty words the matriarch turned and vanished inside the house.

Blair dropped to the back porch steps with a heavy sigh. Mechanically she called out to Danny not to wander too far in his search for more lightning bugs. She remembered when she'd been a collector, stalking the blinking trail like an obsessed bounty hunter. And she remembered even more about those childhood times—the disillusionment when she'd been rejected as a suitable playmate, when it seemed the only purpose she served was to be the brunt of other children's jokes. Maybe Grams had been right. Maybe her act today had been committed as much for the sake of retribution as protectiveness. And maybe the hurt she carried had poisoned rather than toughened her.

Blair raised her eyes to the surrounding dark. Night had closed in. Only the occasional flash of a firefly and a cricket's chirp kept her company. She stood, half-aware that something was amiss. She could no longer see or hear her son. While she'd been lost in the past, he'd wandered out of bounds.

"Dann-eee!" she called, pacing the pitch-black yard. She strained to hear his returning call, but none was forthcoming. She put her hands to her mouth and yelled louder. Again dead silence answered her. Anxiously she strode the perimeter of the brambly thicket bordering Grams's property—searching, chanting his name over and over. The moonless night hindered her vision and only the lowing of Grams's old Jersey responded from the barn. Blair peered into the thicket, its night shadows and sounds alarming her heart. Quickly she pivoted and broke for the house, thoughts of obtaining a flashlight and assistance uppermost in her mind.

The screen door whacked behind her as she tore into the kitchen and began to rummage through drawers for a flashlight. Her hands lighted upon the metal case, but as she clicked it on nothing happened. *Damn!* she cursed beneath her breath, flicking the button back and forth and hitting the lens against her palm. Batteries! Where in the hell did Grams store more batteries? Her hands raked the drawers once more, odds and ends of junk spilling in her frenzy.

"Lordy! Such a racket! What ere you up to now?" Grams bustled into the kitchen, staring at her frantic granddaughter in miffed confusion.

"Danny's missing. I can't find him in the dark . . . need a light . . . maybe help!" The panic in Blair's voice momentarily stunned Grams.

"Batteries, Grams! Help me find some batteries!" Blair's eyes, unduly bright with anxiety, locked with the old woman's. Instantly Grams reached into the back of the drawer and produced the batteries.

"I'll get my shawl," she murmured, hurrying from the room.

Near crazy with worry, Blair fumbled in haste while recharging the flashlight. Once she had accomplished the task, she started for the door, halted, then abruptly turned to stare at the phone. She reached for the receiver, hesitated, but then smothered her pride and placed the call.

"Matt, it's Blair. I need your help. Danny's wandered off in the dark. I've called and called, but he doesn't answer me. I'm afraid he's lost in the thicket." There was a second's pause before she added, "Hurry, please," and slammed down the receiver.

By the time she reached the door again, she had been

joined by a shawled and stony-faced Grams. With a gentle hand upon the old woman's shoulder she tried to soften her rejection. "Really, Grams, I think someone should stay here in case Danny finds his way back." She neglected to mention that Grams's turtle pace would only slow her down.

Grams contemplated the suggestion, then gave an understanding nod. "I'll fire a round if he returns." With a squeeze of her fingertips Blair disappeared into the night's blackness. Grams pursed her lips, thought a moment, then strode to the phone.

"Rev Akins, this here's Grams Logan. I hate botherin' you so late, but we got trouble. Seems that youngun of ours wandered off while chasin' fireflies, 'n' he ain't found his way home yet." She nodded her head while listening to his reply, then ended with "I'd be much obliged," as she hung up, pulled her shawl tighter, and then went to keep a vigil on the backporch.

It was Matt's Cherokee which first screeched to a halt in the driveway, but only seconds later the headlights of Jim Akins's station wagon could be seen in the distance. Matt jumped from the jeep, grabbed his flashlight, and struck out for the thicket.

"They're both in there somewhere," Grams hollered from the porch. "Watch for rattlers. They're bad this time a year."

Matt never replied, plunging into the tangled bramble and getting lost in the maze.

Jim Akins walked up in time to note Matt's direction. He chose an alternate route, reassuring Grams with a calm "Don't worry. We'll find him."

"I'm to fire an all clear when we do," Grams yelled after

him, snuggling deeper inside her shawl and futilely scanning the looming darkness.

Thus the search proceeded—an intense party of three combing inch by inch of dense, treacherous thicket, their flashlights' glow growing dimmer and dimmer in the distance, as an old woman passed the anxious minutes by rocking ceaselessly upon her porch.

Matt moved like a jungle cat through the dense foliage, depending more on his sense of hearing than the limited visibility. He swung a beam of light to his left as an old barn owl hooted, then back to his right as a possum scurried over a log. Every so often he'd stop to call Danny's name or take note of his direction. He'd covered about a mile when he heard what he thought to be a soft whimper only a few yards ahead.

"Danny?" he repeated, aiming the light into the darkness beyond.

"Matt?" came the hushed, tremulous voice.

Suddenly Danny's agonized face appeared in the flashlight's beam. Matt started to rush for him, but froze at the stark terror he encountered in the boy's eyes. Then he heard it—the distinct, chilling sound of a rattle. Cautiously, he eased the light down Danny's small body to the wet and filthy tennis shoes rooted to the ground. There, coiled not two feet away, lay a disturbed and unpredictable rattler. Matt's own eyes dilated with dread.

"Don't move, Danny. Don't even speak. I know it's hard, but you mustn't. Just keep looking at me and breathe easy."

Slowly the rattler uncoiled, slithering closer to Danny. Cautiously Matt reached down for a limb that lay at his feet. The snake inched closer; Matt's hands tightened

119

around the stick. Then, at the last possible moment, Matt made his decision—Danny would be in greater jeopardy unless he acted. Some inner instinct told him that the odds were against his killing the snake before it struck. It was the hardest decision of his life.

"Look at *me*, Danny," he repeated. "Don't move a muscle."

The rattler undulated over Danny's sneakers, its head cocked, only the sound of its agitated rattling filling the still night air. Matt held his breath and forced Danny's obedience with his eyes. "It's nearly over," he whispered. "Stay very still." A lifetime passed before the horny tail of the rattler cleared and then blended with the underbrush.

Matt opened his arms, his voice cracking as he ordered, "Now, boy! Come to me now!" Danny rushed for safety, sobbing pitifully as Matt crushed him close and smoothed his hair. "You're a brave one," Matt said comfortingly.

His arms still wrapped about his rescuer's waist, Danny crooked his neck to stare up at him with tear-filled eyes. "I was so scared, Matt. And I've lost my mason jar full of fireflies." Matt clutched him near once more, thinking how much greater the loss might have been.

"Come on, let's head for home. Your mom's near sick with worry." With a guiding hand on the boy's shoulder, he led the way. At first they progressed at a moderate clip, but soon Danny's weary lag slowed them to a snail's pace.

"Tired?" Matt asked.

Danny gave a reluctant nod. He hated not being able to keep up with his champion.

Matt stopped and squatted down. "Hoist yourself up here, and I'll give you a piggyback."

"I'm too big!" Danny argued.

"You're not so big yet, boy," Matt coaxed with a per-suading tilt of his head. Danny didn't have to be offered twice. Thankfully he climbed aboard.

"One more thing . . ." Matt straightened up and felt Danny's arms tighten about his neck. "I think it'd be better if we kept this snake episode to ourselves for a while. No sense upsetting your mother any more than she already is."

"Okay, Matt. Whatever you say," the boy mumbled, his head drooping listlessly against his rescuer's back. "And, Matt?" he sighed as his heavy eyelids began to close.

"Yeah?"

"Thanks!"

Danny never even heard the fervent "Your welcome" as he drifted into a contented drowse. Reaching up and securing Danny's entwined hands in his own, Matt bal-anced his weight and continued the trek in silence. As he cleared the thicket and stepped into Grams's yard, the old woman sprung to her feet and hustled down the steps. She stood for a composing moment, the drawn look upon her weathered face melting into a broad, relieved smile. When she spoke, the harshness of her words was tempered by the loving concern reflected in her gaze.

"I ought to tan that bad youngun good."

Remembering the sting of Grams's switchings, Matt interceded with a persuasive grin. "Perhaps you should save meting out punishment for in morning. The boy's given out."

"You're certain he's all right?" As if to assure herself, Grams's gnarled hand patted the boy's curls.

"He's fine. Just a little frightened and a lot tired."

"Well, don't just stand there like a blame donkey. Let's get him in the house and tucked in his bed." Grams led the way, bustling and grumbling every step. "It's where he shoulda been hours ago . . . keepin' us all near crazy with worry . . . gonna wale him good come mornin'."

Matt followed into the knotty-pine bedroom, gently laying the lad down on the poster bed and beginning to take off his soiled sneakers.

"Here now, I'll be doin' that." A compulsive giver who needed to be needed, Grams usurped the chore. "You look about as tuckered as him. Do one more service, then fetch a jug of my homemade cider from the pantry and set yourself to rest on the back porch."

Matt submitted without argument. "What is it you want me to do?"

"Fire a round into the air so's Blair and the Rev know you found him. That hardheaded gal would lose herself afore givin' up the search. Why, if she thought any harm befell the boy, you might just as well bury her." Bent over Danny, Grams did not see the anguished look that fleeted across Matt's haggard face. Compulsively he reached to brush Danny's hair from his forehead but, lightning-quick, Grams slapped his hand away.

"Don't be wakin' him, Matthew! And do as I tell you!" she admonished, carefully disguising the perceptive gleam which lit her wise old eyes.

Knowing better than to buck her, Matt did as he was told. Retrieving the jug from the pantry and the shotgun from its rack on the sittin' room wall, he returned to the porch. After firing a shattering blast into the night sky, he then worked the cork free with his teeth and took a long,

122

much-needed pull. Revived and rewarded, he sank to the porch steps, set the jug between his knees, and awaited the rest of the search party's return.

Many sips and minutes later Blair emerged from the thicket. Watching her sprint across the yard, Matt was reminded of the tomboy he had once known. When she reached him, panting, her clothes snagged and hair disarrayed, he immediately noted the angry scratch that marked her cheek. He had a inexplicable urge to run his finger along its red length and and soothe away her ache.

"Danny," she panted. "Is he. . . . ?" Her dazed eyes met his, and she knew the answer. "Thank God," she whispered, her entire body slumping as her eyes closed against an onslaught of tears.

Matt reached for her, his strong arms guiding her numb weight to the steps beside him. "He's exhausted, but otherwise just fine. Grams is putting him to bed. Here, have a sip. At the moment it's you who looks the worse for wear."

Blindly she followed his advice, the bite of the cider revitalizing her spent body. Her head rested languidly against the railing as a long moment of silence passed between them. "I thanked God, but I've yet to thank you," she said at last.

Reflexively Matt's fingertip traced the angry scrape along her cheekbone. "No thanks necessary, Mrs. Hayden. I treasure that boy almost as much as you." For a beautiful but fleeting instant, their deepest, sweetest memories were revisited—a long-ago summer, an unforgettable touch, and a mood never to be recaptured.

"Hey!" Jim Akins's voice echoed from the edge of the

thicket. "So, the stray has returned." Instantly Matt drew back as Blair stiffened.

"Yes, Jim," she confirmed. "Come join us." She glanced at Matt, who sat quiet and impassive until Jim sauntered up, whereupon he held out the jug to him. There seemed something challenging in the gesture.

"Yes, join us, Rev. We're having a sort of celebration." For some odd reason Blair didn't completely trust Matt's easy smile. Jim Akins, however, seemed totally unreadable.

"I don't usually indulge, but I think tonight's success dictates that we imbibe."

A wisp of a smirk crossed Matt's lips as he relinquished the jug. "I heartily concur, Rev." His reply sounded a little too agreeable to Blair's mind.

She looked from one to the other, wondering at the strange undercurrents she sensed. Rev Akins slumped to a step beneath her and hoisted the jug to his lips. A satisfied "Ahhh" escaped him as he graciously offered her a turn at the cider. Not to be outdone by a couple of jousting men, she chugged a sip, then passed the jug to Matt with the excuse of checking on her son. She left the two of them exchanging quips and sips and mellowing at an extraordinary pace. When she returned, she couldn't quite distinguish whether if it was her imagination or reality that made them both appear to be drawling their words.

"I felt all along that the boy wasn't in any real danger," the reverend was saying. "Merely exercising his preadolescent rebelliousness."

"That a fact?" Matt scowled. "Well, I tell ya, Rev, anytime a person wanders into those woods, there's an element of danger present." The jug exchanged hands once more.

"Well, at least it didn't confront us tonight. The Lord protects the innocent and young." Jim Akins smiled warmly as Blair joined them on the steps.

Matt resented his words almost as much as the affectionate hand he extended to Blair. He'd been pumping the good reverend full of potent cider, hoping to dispense with his company, and all he'd gotten for his efforts was a drinking, lingering rival. Besides which, Matt was fed up with listening to child psychology and spiritual rhetoric. He had more important things on his mind—like the feel of Blair's skin and shape of her mouth. Tonight he felt a bond—one which had never completely been severed and that still joined him to Blair. But the reverend kept talking and chugging, cooing and wooing. Enough! He had had enough! Matt hauled himself to his feet with a longing look in Blair's direction.

"I suppose I should be heading on home. I have a mare about to foal, and I always make it a point to check on her before turning in."

Blair caught Jim's gloating expression. Could it be that the guileless reverend suspected Matt's intentions and had craftily set out to beat him at his own game? As she got up, her departing glance at Matt seconded his frustration. "I thank you again. I don't know what we'd have done without your help." She held out her hand, which he enclosed firmly and needily.

"Blair . . . I . . ." Uncharacteristically Matt floundered. Never could he express the secret yearning buried deep in his heart. He gazed deep into her eyes, pressed her hand, then quickly withdrew. "I'm glad it all turned out so well." His tall figure soon blended with the moonless night.

Blair sank to the steps and stared into the darkness. She was hardly aware of it when Jim's head cradled against her knee.

"I'm glad too, Blair," he softly said. "I can't bear to see you upset or dismayed." Her hand started to light upon his golden head, but then the old warning of Luke rang in her head—never again must she naively misinterpret a man's tenderness. She rejected the impulse and sighed.

"I know you're tired, and I won't keep you much longer." Jim's head lifted. In silent homage his deep blue eyes adored her. Then, slowly, purposefully, his hand nestled the back of her neck and pulled her lips to his. His kiss was unexpectedly experienced, yet unbelievably gentle. She couldn't wound him by resisting, nor would she encourage him by responding.

"I love you, Blair" came his murmured declaration against her lips. "I think I've loved the thought of you always; it's just that I had yet to find you." His eyes never left her face as she eased his hand from around her neck, then tenderly enfolded it within her own.

"Please, Jim, don't say these things. Neither the image you have of me nor the future you imagine between us is real. I don't want to hurt or mislead you. So, I have to tell you that . . ."

His resolve was as strong as his feelings for her, and he postponed her rejection by pressing a fingertip to her lips. "Give me a chance," he pleaded. "I'm not asking for anything more. Often time can make the difference between what actually is and what might be. *We can be,*

126

Blair if you'll only just let us." Before she could collect herself to the point of responding, he stood, smiled, and then opportunely strode out the gate.

She sat immobile, shrouded in the night's shadows, and appalled by her own clumsiness. Was it only her extreme moodiness, or did history seem to be repeating itself?

CHAPTER EIGHT

After reassuring herself one last time that Danny was sleeping safe and sound in his bed, a restless and reflective Blair set out on a back-road hike. Hands in pockets and her thoughts out of control, she followed an aimless course. Once again Jim had resurrected the ghosts of men who'd shared and shaped her life. Then, as now, she'd been faced with the dilemma of whether to grasp the security of a kind and loving suitor, or to pack up her dreams and wander further away from the one man who'd never commit himself.

Years ago fate had been kind and presented Jess like an answer to a prayer. He was older, wiser, and had no delusions about what he had to offer or stood to gain. Their honest relationship deprived them of neither. In fact, in totally separate ways, their marriage provided stability for both. But a miracle such as Jess only happened once. Unlike her deceased husband, Jim more closely resembled the romantic Luke. It seemed as if her life had come full circle. Once more Blair found herself facing a familiar decision—whether to temporarily or permanently dash another sensitive admirer's romantic hopes. Somehow she always found herself pursued by men whose love she couldn't fully return.

But why couldn't she? her rational self argued. For years she'd withheld that part of herself which might have fulfilled her as a woman. For what? For the sake of a man and a moment that existed only as memories? When did one decide to store away their unattainable dreams like sentimental momentoes too precious to destroy, but too painful to keep in view? Though Blair's mind still pondered the questions, her heart stubbornly rejected the answers. On this night love was to have its way.

Without her preoccupied mind's consent her heart led her to where she wished to be—the Farrett stables. Like a beckoning beam, a crack of light shining from under the stable door lured her onward. Not yet fully comprehending why, but unable to stop herself, Blair entered.

Half-dazed, she gazed dumbfoundedly at Matt. He sat upon a bale of hay, indulging in additional cider with a tinge of despair. As their eyes met and held, a palpable tension was transmitted between them.

"Why'd you come, Blair? Did the preacher boy disappoint you?" Matt's semi-intoxicated state caused his speech to be blunt.

She shifted uneasily. "Don't be cruel, Matt. I'm really not up to it tonight."

With a shrug he lowered his mocking eyes. "Sorry, but to tell you the truth, I'm not exactly myself at the moment. Care for a sip?" At the condescending shake of her head he smirked indifferently, then saluted her with the jug before taking another drink. "I guess you realize he's in love with you. It's written all over him. But then, I don't suppose that surprises you very much. Surely by now you've grown accustomed to men making fools of themselves over you?" Though liquor tainted the words, it was jealous longing which inspired them.

Realizing the danger of Matt's sarcastic mood and her

vulnerability to his persecution, Blair turned to leave. In one swift motion he sprung, slamming the door shut and pinning her between his outspread arms. She flattened against the door, silently pleading for release with her alarmed eyes.

"I repeat, Blair," he badgered. "Why'd you come?" The faint sweetness of liquor on his breath explained his lack of tact.

Evasively she lowered her eyes. "I was restless . . . out walking . . . I saw your light . . ." She groped for a plausible excuse.

"No, Blair," he murmured, his fingers gliding through her hair, then tugging lightly until he had forced her eyes to meet his. "You were out walking . . . remembering . . . and suddenly you felt compelled to be with me." He began to weave the silky strands between his fingertips, slowly, communicatively.

Her skin tingled with each electric touch. "Please, Matt, don't do this. I'm weary of the game. I don't want to hurt, or be hurt anymore."

The sadness in her voice drew his hands to her shoulders. With an easy motion he pulled her close against him. She felt the stifled sigh that escaped from deep within his chest. "I think our fears are mutual. This past hour all I've been able to do is sit here, stare into space, and try to drown all thoughts of you in homemade liquor."

His hands began to explore her back in meandering caresses. "We both know why you came; you wanted it and I willed it." His body melted closer, his lips tracing short, enticing kisses to her anticipating mouth. "Dear God! How I've wanted you," he confessed, his voice

130

husky, near grieving. "This moment may hurt us both, but for all the empty ones can't we chance it?"

In unspoken answer her lips claimed his in a fevered kiss. *A moment . . . chance it . . . for all the empty ones . . .* Her mind repeated his plea as her heart echoed his need. Matt groaned beneath her responsive mouth, his arms crushing her even closer against the stimulating length of him as his tongue sought hers and heightened the ecstasy. The passion of a hundred dreams, a thousand lost hours, exploded with a fervor that consumed them both. As Matt released her mouth to trail the slim curve of her neck with the moist tip of his tongue, she moaned incoherently.

"Say you need me as much as I do you."

"I thought I had," he rasped.

"Please, please, mean it, Matt," she breathlessly begged.

"I do, tomboy. I do," he murmured, half-crazy with the sweet smell, sweet taste, sweet feel of her. His fingers moved with precision as they removed her blouse, undid her lace bra, and slipped it from her ivory shoulders. His hands felt masterful, pleasurable, as they cupped her breasts and massaged them to ripened fullness. She sighed deeply, her head lolling backward as he drew one taut nipple, then the other, into his warm, anxious mouth, relaxing them to full bloom with the hypnotic rotation of his tongue.

Her hands slipped under his shirt to knead the flesh of his back, then slowly glided down his sleek sides until they moved forward and raked the manly fur upon his chest. Her fingers trembled with desire as she unfastened the buttons of his shirt, then pressed a cheek against his firm abdomen. Suggestively her lips smoothed the light-brown line that disappeared beneath his jeans. A shudder traveled down his entire body as her tapered nails ran along the inside of the denim waistband, then unsnapped the catch and eased them down his long, lean legs.

She was out of her mind with need. If there was to be just once, then let it be a once in a lifetime. Matt was mesmerized as she dropped to her knees and began to trip light kisses along his inner thighs.

"Sorceress!" He grabbed her shoulders, drawing her upright, and kicking off the jeans all in one motion. As his crystal-blue eyes locked with hers, all the words that had gone unsaid were spoken—"I've missed you, I've longed for you, I need you."

The moment was out of control; they were beyond reason. There would be no beautiful foreplay, no reassurances, no adult games. Their need was too great. An insatiable hunger had to be satisfied first—a hunger that years couldn't diminish or circumstance abolish. For theirs were two souls yoked, two hearts bound, two lives pledged.

Fiercely Matt claimed her mouth as he swung her up into his arms. She clutched his neck tightly, deepening the intensity of his kiss. Both were oblivious to where his footsteps led—an end stall, a pile of fresh hay. Only release mattered; not where, or how, or why. Matt's strong arms eased her to the bed of hay. His own hands trembled as he removed her jeans, then slipped her scanty underwear down her shapely legs and over polished toes. After shedding his own briefs, he knelt beside her, and for a breathless, suspended moment his eyes worshiped the feminine beauty they beheld.

"A man would be a fool not to savor you." He groaned,

his palm gliding from her shoulder, across the firm swell of her breasts, along the flat of her stomach, then down a satin thigh. His eyes hazed with desire, and she knew and shared his torment.

"I don't want to be savored, Matt," she whispered hoarsely. "I've waited so long for you." Shining auburn hair spread upon sheaves of hay, alluring golden eyes, open arms, and a body arched in anticipation, obliterated his restraint. His muscular legs straddled her and, with a surge born of a decade of yearning, he cleaved to her.

Their union was torrid and musky, a sequence of thrusts and tears, moans and rapture. An exorcism of past hurt, it was also the conception of new joy. In an earthy setting they found heavenly fulfillment while in each other they rediscovered that part of themselves that had long been lost, but now was whole. When she cried his name at the summit of their passion, he answered with a tenderness that allayed her doubts. Matt was hers once more—maybe not forever, but for now.

And when that night they again made love, the fever in their souls ebbed. For now the moment was at hand to savor, to adore, to truly grow to know each other; not just of the flesh, but of the heart. They touched and actually felt; spoke and really heard. The night and their world was comprised of many wonders—the sweet smell of summer and passion's scent upon entwined bodies, the sound of a distant whippoorwill and the synchronized beat of two hearts, the silver reflection of distant stars and the amber glow beheld in a lover's gaze. But most wondrous of all was the miracle of lying beside the one you love, to feel each drawn breath, and know the dreams they weave.

Such were Blair's thoughts as she lie cradled in Matt's arms while awaiting the first dawning light.

Clad only in his shirt, she snuggled closer for warmth. Her lips brushed his shoulder, and he stirred. As she lifted her head to free his cramped arm, he rolled away from her onto his side. She smiled at his boyish position—knees drawn up, his hands tucked between them. Adoringly her palm grazed his bare back. Then with a tapered nail she airily traced the invisible vow *I love you, Matt* upon his smooth skin. She sighed contentedly, draped one arm over him, and closed her eyes. She hardly felt him move as his hand caught hers and drew her fingertips to his lips. Like her, his declaration went unspoken. For between lovers a sensual silence is always heard.

CHAPTER NINE

Never before had summer days been as special, summer nights so wonderful as those shared by Blair and Matt. During the day their laughter rang lighter than Ozark sunshine while at night their soft love words mingled with the hush of the hills. They were children again—romping wild-flowered meadows, skipping rocks over babbling brooks, climbing Old Baldy. They were lovers once more —discovering, sharing, uniting. They were young, but mature; carefree, yet committed. *They were in love.*

It was another of those unforgettable nights, when a tepid breeze billowed the curtains on Matt's bedroom window and silvery moonlight gleamed across the room to swathe their naked flesh, that Blair and Matt sanctioned their love once more—a love as bountiful as a harvest at a perfect season's end; as fresh as the earth after a sudden rain. Every touch, each look they exchanged, expressed a sentiment long denied a voice, yet now silently confided.

Matt lay stretched upon his side, his covetous blue eyes following the lazy meander of his fingertip as he traced his beloved's profile. She was beyond a doubt the most beautiful woman he'd ever known—her color vibrant, sensual to the touch, and perfectly formed. He stroked her sleek throat, feeling as much as hearing her guttural purr. She reminded him of an independent feline—lithe, instinctive, and territorial. His hand moved to the swell of her breasts,

135

savoring their soft rise and fall with each sigh she breathed. God! How he loved the feel of her—every memorized inch. He rose slightly to brush his cheek along the satin plane of her stomach. He heard her delighted moan as her body stretched, then writhed beneath him. Slowly his lips traveled her flawless skin, heightening, intensifying her response.

Her fingers meshed within his sun-streaked hair, guiding, repeating his seductive trail. And when his tongue glided down the divide of her breasts, then fanned the raging fire that blazed lower, then lower still, she rasped his name in a voice that begged and commanded all at once. "Please, Matt . . ." came her fevered entreaty.

"What would please you?" he urged, his soothing hands quelling the tremor in her thighs. His fingers moved upward to begin a suggestive kneading of her hips. She closed her eyes and flowed with the undulating movement.

Provocatively her tongue moistened her dry lips as she whispered, "Having you . . . now and always."

Five meaningful words coupled with a beguiling look unleashed latent passion and brought his hard body upon her soft one. Hungrily her hands cradled the back of his head, pressing his nurturing mouth to hers in unashamed greed. She drew the honey from his kiss, her tongue plundering the sweet depth of his mouth and pillaging his senses. A dew of passion covered their bodies as flesh frictioned against flesh, then became one.

Matt matched his pace to hers, quickening and deepening his thrusts with each arch and writhe of her body. Her nails marked his back as her need reached its peak, then prolonged the euphoria. Oh, but she could drive a man wild . . . She was magic—trances and mist, infinity and

136

bliss. With her a man knew that he pleased and satisfied, but more than this she promised a fulfillment which would survive the evanescent moment.

Her arms encircled him, weaving him even deeper within her silken spell. The drum of her irregular heartbeat blended with intoxicating scent of lilac upon her skin. Her lips brushed his sensitive ear, whispering love chants, revealing secret desires. And as her hands roamed his body and her lips enticed him to follow her beyond the confines of a narrow bed, a cloistered room, a shallow world, his blue eyes glazed with the wonder of her. She became a rainbow of ardor—flowing copper hair, shimmering green eyes, rose lips, and cream skin; a haze of motion—tender caresses, expressive sighs, wild kisses, and seductive moves. For this incomparable, incoherent moment only hues and motion filled his world, and only Blair could fulfill his need. They had no past, maybe no future, but they had the sensual splendor, the fragile miracle, of here and now.

"Follow me," her eyes told him as she pressed him flat against the tangled sheets and wooed him with an enchanting smile. "Trust me," her kiss assured him as she lowered her willowy body onto him and slowly led the way to love's limbo. "Love me, love me, love me," her tears begged him, as she intoned the plea, at first sensitively, then fiercely.

And he did as she beckoned, loving her until her tears and his passion subsided. Long hours afterward, with the salt of her tears pungent upon his lips, he cradled her in his sheltering arms and shielded her against the morning's doubts. He'd fight heaven and earth to preserve the remainder of the night's magic till dawn.

* * *

"He's here! Hurry, Mom, he's here!" Danny burst out the screen door in a flurry of excitement. As fast as his legs could carry him, he ran to meet the Cherokee pulling into the drive. He kept pace alongside, holding onto the door handle and rapidly firing questions in the window at Matt.

"Did you bring the inner tube? How about the snorkel?"

"Got it all." Matt grinned, braked, and opened the door.

"Don't get out!" Danny warned, nearly slamming the door shut on Matt's legs. "If you get out, they'll want to offer you coffee and all that stuff. We'll only be that much later getting started."

Remembering his own impatience as a boy, Matt nodded his complete understanding. Danny scurried around the front of the Cherokee, then plopped his body beside his co-conspirator to await his dawdling mother.

"Women!" he scoffed. "Always wasting time. Why does she have to comb her dumb old hair anyway? It's just gonna get all wet when she jumps into the spring. Makes no sense."

"I take it you didn't bother to comb yours?" Matt settled back in the seat with a nonchalant air.

"Heck, no!" The boy fidgeted beneath his suddenly censorious gaze. "But I will," he added hastily. "Right after we finish swimming." His anxious hazel eyes darted to the door as his mother stepped out upon the porch. Like a mischievous monkey, he scampered over Matt to yell out the window. "Matt's in a *real* big hurry, Mom." He started at the reprimanding swat Matt landed on his backside. Edging sheepishly back to his center post, he checked an impish smirk as Blair joined them in the jeep.

138

"Sorry." She smiled apologetically as she placed the picnic basket beneath her feet.

"When a woman looks as fresh and pretty as you, an apology is unnecessary. The time was well spent." Matt winked as he started the motor, she beamed, while Danny crossed his arms over his chest, sinking deeper against the seat and rolling his eyes disgustedly.

The midmorning sun's sweltering glare had already wilted the countryside. In local dialect, the day would be termed a scorcher. The Cherokee stirred a haze of dust as it proceeded along the gravel road leading toward the dippin' spring. Blair ran a forearm across her brow, then leaned closer to the open window to catch a wisp of breeze. Her eyes trailed to Matt, chatting and laughing with Danny. He showed no ill effects from so little sleep. In fact, he appeared to be rejuvenated—almost as boyishly enthusiastic as his son. *His son!* How easily her thoughts admitted his right, and how deceitfully she concealed the fact. The stagnant mugginess within the jeep was suffocating, much like her guilt.

How could she make love to this man by night, then cheat him of the knowledge of his son by day? What kind of a woman was she—conniving as Matt had accused, or cautious, as she would prefer to believe? Could weeks of intimacy erase years of mistrust? Damn! Why must she wrestle with so much for so very long? Unlike Matt, she was bone-weary, and it showed. But then, Matt didn't harbor a burdensome secret which day by day, year by year, stole his peace and drained his soul. Thoughtlessly Blair's hand wiped at the moisture collecting at the deep plunging V of her swimsuit.

"A cool dip will feel refreshing." Though Matt directed

139

his comment quite generally, the angle of his glance remained very pointed. He noted Danny's eager nod but, more importantly, he recorded the absence of Blair's reply. She was lost in deep thought again—the same as on that day they'd all shared lunch at Farrett House. He sensed the similarity of her mood. Something very personal and serious grieved her. Something she couldn't or wouldn't confide, not even after all they'd shared. The realization wounded Matt, but his pride prevented him from asking. He knew from his own darker self that some hurts must be borne alone. It wasn't an act of bravery or stubbornness; it was merely an unalterable fact.

The Cherokee drew to halt beneath the shade of a weeping willow. Nothing would do for Danny but to unload and go for a dip immediately. Matt cast Blair a quizzical look, but she merely shrugged her shoulders and gave in to her impetuous son's demands. As she spread the picnic blanket under the willow Matt followed the gleeful Danny to the crystal cool water's edge. Blair watched as the two shed their shirts, then raced each other in. The sight was both comical and sad—for they looked like frolicking puppies, yet the similarity between father and son was remarkable. Blair looked away as she stripped out of her shorts, then lay prone upon the blanket to stare up at the blue, blue sky.

She pictured another memorable picnic—an excursion for two young lovers on a hot summer's day. On that occasion the sky shone indigo, like today, while the sun's warmth dried two spirited bodies after an impulsive skinny dip. The lovers were she and Matt; the day marked Danny's conception. This she knew as surely as the ring of her son's laughter floating up from the spring's edge.

Matt had loved her then—loved her with the brashness and awkwardness of youth.

And, oh, how she had loved him—his ease, his style, his smile. Dear God! How she still loved him—his strength, his pride, and forever his smile. But love was much simpler back then—reckless and wild. Only through time, mistakes, and hurt did lovers learn to test and mistrust. It was such a sad revelation to discover that loving someone didn't necessarily insure happiness, and that many times the strongest of loves can be shattered by the smallest doubt.

A shadow fell across her tranced face, and she blinked to stare up at Matt. He knelt beside her for a reflective moment, his palm smoothing the pensive crease on her forehead.

"You're frowning, and that's definitely not allowed," he murmured.

"I'm not," she replied in a teasing tone. "I was just squinting."

He cocked his head dubiously, his clear blue eyes reminding her of the indigo sky. Only Danny's demanding call for the inner tube saved her.

"I'll be back shortly, and you'd better be smiling," he warned. Much too quickly and obediently she flashed him a devastating grin. He quirked a skeptical brow as he reluctantly retreated. Several times he turned back to check on her while making his way to the spring. Only after he had completely disappeared from view did Blair release the sigh she stifled.

He loved her then, but did he love her now? The crucial question kept repeating in her head. Did she dare believe he'd understand her years of silence? Did she have the right to gamble three futures on a supreme test of love? What if it all backfired—Matt hating her more than either of them thought possible and, in revenge, claiming the missed ten years with their son? Blair buried her head in her hands, unable to bear the horrible thought. She might lose everything that ever held meaning in her life—the only man who'd truly fulfilled her, and a cherished son.

"Oh, God, what should I do?" she silently lamented, hugging her knees tightly to her chest and rocking miserably to fight off the waves of panic overwhelming her. No answer was forthcoming. As always, no one was going to intercede in her behalf. It was up to the hickory hillbilly to cope. She ran the back of her hand over her eyes, took a deep breath, and collected herself. Falling apart at this moment wouldn't solve anything. She must save her strength for a test that would present itself all too soon.

Blair busied herself with needlessly rearranging the contents of the picnic basket, then rose and climbed the steep grade to the old oak. She stood high above it all, looking down on the two ruffians playfully dumping each other from the inner tube. Their laughter was a catharsis. The dread lifted from her heart and a soft smile formed on her lips as she returned Danny's wave.

"Watch, Mom," he yelled. "Matt taught me how to dive through the center of the ring."

"Okay, let's see your stuff, hotshot," she challenged, thinking how wonderful it was to witness each small triumph he accomplished. So engrossed was she in Danny's achievement that she paid no heed to Matt's stealthy assault of the bluff. Abruptly her admiring clap and words of praise ended as Matt swung on the tree rope, lurched

142

her up from behind, and carried her screaming and kicking into the water below.

She emerged sputtering and fuming to Danny's elated giggles and Matt's devilish grin. "Oh, you're going to pay for that one, Matthew Farrett," she muttered.

"Am I?" he replied, leaning back into a float, as if her threat held little consequence. "I think city life's made you soft, Blair." He prodded a bit more, watching out of the corner of his eye as she strategically maneuvered closer.

"Well, this city gal can still stand up to you," she scoffed, lunging for him, the momentum of her body taking them both under the water.

Matt came up with her in his arms and, with a mighty heave, sent her sprawling back beneath the water. She bobbed to the surface, wrapping her arms about his neck and hauling him under once more.

As they surfaced, Danny's squeals of delight joined the chaos. "Get him, Mom! That-a-boy, Matt!" His fickle allegiance switched to whoever happened to be winning at the moment.

Matt clamped one hand on the top of Blair's head and shoved her under again. She came up under his legs, knocking him off balance and sending him toppling. They became a tangle of arms and legs, breathless pants, and churning water.

"Say enough!" Matt demanded.

"You first!" she countered.

Water and bodies collided once more. This time the two combatants disappeared from sight, and Danny bit his lip as the seconds passed. Little did he know that Matt had bear-hugged his mother and was kissing her into submission while obscured from his curious view. At last they surfaced—breathless, spent, and clinging.

"Had enough?" Matt grinned, curbing an urge to crush her even closer.

Her eyes sparked with passion and mischief. "I never get enough," she laughed, catching him off guard and dunking him a last time before she swam.

"She tricked you, Matt!" The innocent Danny could not believe his mother's wiliness. "Don't let her get away with it."

Matt grinned his intent, then set out to overtake her. It was a mad dash for shore, but Blair scrambled up the bank and ran for the willow first. Matt caught her just as they reached the picnic blanket. His arms wrapped about her waist, and they tumbled to the quilt entwined and laughing.

"Do you give in?" he murmured, his lips nuzzling her temple coercively.

She brushed her fingertips over his mouth in unmistakable suggestion. "Ask me nicely, and I might."

"You're shameless, Blair Logan." He nipped her fingertips. "Offering me bribes when you know I can't take them." He glanced meaningfully toward the spring, then forced his yearning body upright and grabbed for a towel. His arousing touch as he wiped the crystal droplets from her skin ignited a sensual ripple deep within. She leaned back on her palms and closed her eyes. As the towel looped about her neck and drew her petal-soft lips to his, a remembrance of that hot summer day long ago crept over her. Some things never change—the sun felt warm, his kiss heavenly, as she drifted in déjà-vu.

"I think that rebel streak is what I *once* loved most in

144

you, Blair." His casual remark jolted her. She dare not meet his gaze for fear of revealing the total desolation mirrored in her eyes. His gentle smoothing of her hair had barely registered before he vanished back to the spring and Danny. She sat transfixed, a sudden foreboding chill stealing across her flesh. She wrapped the towel tighter around herself and stared in the direction of their roughhousing shouts.

The word *once* echoed over and over in her mind, like *once-upon-a-time* and *they-lived-happily-ever-after*. Surely the past few weeks had been more than just a nostalgic replay of a fairy tale romance never meant to be. Surely fate couldn't be so cruel as to allow her to forfeit her heart once more only to have it broken again. *Once* was not enough! God only knew how much more she craved!

The premonition of doom which taunted Blair followed her into the night. It loomed between her and Matt as they lay together. She was desperate to keep him near, to seal their love so it might never be taken from them again. Laden with fear and guilt, her thoughts in a turmoil and her plan unclear, she clung to him with a misery that was impossible to ignore.

Anxious and attuned to her mood, Matt held her close and stroked her hair soothingly. Tonight she seemed like a starving child reaching out to him. Her arms tightened about his neck and her body pressed near, as if seeking sustenance. He sheathed her needy flesh with his and sought to comfort her in silent ways. He, too, sensed the inevitable end of magic and the return of reality.

"Matt," she whispered. "We've got to talk."

"I know," he sighed, pushing aside the stray auburn strands that wisped her pale face.

She kissed the muscular arm that lay beneath her head. "There's a memory between us, darling." She felt his sinuous flex and her heart constricted. "He's with us, Matt, every hour of every day, like the invisible air we breathe. We can't deny his existence."

Matt withdrew his arm, lay still, and stared blankly at the ceiling. "Don't do this, Blair . . . not now, not tonight." His words held a kind of foreboding that coiled around her throat and strangled her reply. She cradled her head on his chest, feeling the slow, dirgelike beat of his heart. It had to be said. His name had to be spoken. If she was to change *once* into forever, the question of Luke had to be discussed and resolved. Visions of herself professing her innocence in Luke's eventual fate, of convincing Matt that her only guilt was one of naiveté when it came to understanding men, of, maybe even, proclaiming Danny's true parentage, encouraged her next words.

Her hand nestled his cheek, forcing his obstinate eyes to hers. "Matt, don't you see, we're living in a fool's paradise. Luke *was* and *is* an essential part of our lives." She froze at his instantaneous and melancholy withdrawal. He sat up on the edge of the bed, his shoulders slumped, his back turned to her. "Matt?" Her fingertips grazed his back imploringly. He made no move toward her. There only came a dismal shake of his head.

"Why, Blair?" he choked. "Why did you have to present us with our guilt all over again? Don't you realize that by saying his name you've reopened the old wounds? I've been trying to deal with it. Why couldn't you?" His fingers raked his hair as he buried his head in his hands.

"Because it's wrong and self-defeating, darling." She inched toward him, wrapping her arms around his waist and trailing his back with an apologetic kiss. He stiffened and broke free from her. He crossed to the window, thoughtfully gazing out upon the land which Luke could no longer see, smell, or walk.

"Ten years seems like such a long, long time," he murmured. "I was wrong to have let my pride separate us. I was young, indecisive, and impressionable. I still cared what people thought. You were taboo, Blair. Everyone said so. And I wasn't man enough to admit publicly my love for the notorious Blair Logan." His hands clutched each side of the window facing, the streaming moonlight etching the agony upon his face. "Luke, though, he was different—swift and sure. He had no qualms about acknowledging his fondness for you. I couldn't help being jealous of his conviction and his feelings toward you. I died a little inside each time I knew he was meeting you . . . loving you . . . taking you away from me."

"Matt, I . . ." She tried to explain the innocence of Luke's devotion.

"No, let me finish," he continued. "Then I decided he was the better man. He deserved to have you. I reconciled myself to his good fortune. All these years I've carried the guilt of hesitating, then the shame of coveting the love that befell my brother. But you . . ." He turned to face her, his eyes prisms of ice, his words even colder. "Your guilt is betrayal. You betrayed all three of us when you accepted Luke's consolation, and then ran away like a coward when you couldn't commit yourself. And Danny . . ."

His voice trailed off as he returned to the window and focused on the hollow that nestled the boy. "What have we passed on to him, woman? How are we to overcome the sorrow of it all?" His voice broke as a suppressed groan racked his body.

How indeed? her logical self echoed. She ached to comfort him, but the confession caught in her throat. He was so proud, so hurt, so wrong. And yet, deep in her heart she knew Matt could not withstand hearing the truth at this moment. The sheer hypocrisy of it all would break him—the wasted years, the needless pain. No, now was not the time, if ever. For if he hesitated again, her love could not survive the rejection. In truth, she couldn't fully trust his reaction; she wouldn't blindly believe in the man she loved. And this was *her* shame.

Slowly she climbed from the bed and slipped into her clothes. She stood for a paralytic moment, her sorrowful eyes memorizing the window-framed portrait of the tormented lover she adored; the same man who'd once before forsaken her. Her heart breaking and silent tears streaming down her cheeks, she eased over to Matt's side, then wordlessly slid an arm around his waist.

Possessively he clutched his precious tomboy close. "I'd give anything . . . everything . . . if we could overcome the past." He wept the bitterness she could not shed. She was his pillar of strength, no sobs, no pleas, no confession, only a parting kiss and a whispered, remorseful vow.

"Maybe one day we can forgive each other our pride. I love you, Matt . . . now and always."

CHAPTER TEN

Unlike Blair's grief, time passed. The weeks of September dispelled the heat wave as thoroughly as Matt had dashed her dreams. As she sat rocking lethargically on the back porch, her thoughts rustled like the constant murmur of fall leaves. Her pensive eyes looked beyond the valley, beyond summer and love. For though she had hoped the prideful gap between her and Matt might be bridged, she really no longer believed it possible. They'd maintained a yearning distance, an alienating silence. It seemed that fate had decreed they would share no more than Danny. Maybe, in truth, the child was all that was destined to prevail—the only lasting happiness they'd ever receive from one another. Resignedly Blair closed her eyes. Lost in despair, she never heard her grandmother's approach.

"Harvestin' your thoughts agin?" The matriarch's voice held subtle concern as she crossed to the railing and scanned the ripe fields.

"Merely resting." Blair followed her gaze.

"You know, honey, sometimes a crop can suffer from too much tendin'. Some things jest got to run their natural course—take for instance a fast stream, the change of seasons, or a confused man." She emphasized the last words, never turning to meet her granddaughter's eyes. "You think I don't know you're grievin'. Well, you're wrong, cause I do. I've seen sorrow in my days, mine and

149

others. Gets so a person can mark sufferin' on a face and hear ache in a voice. You got all the signs."

"Grams." Blair sighed, rising from the rocker and coming to rest on the railing beside the old woman. "I'm coping and, given some time, I'll survive." Reassuringly, she squeezed her grandmother's bony hand. "It's just that with each disappointment it gets a little bit harder to pretend it doesn't matter." A betraying quiver of her chin brought Grams's arms around her. The consoling gesture completely broke down Blair's reserve. She buried her head against the familiar bosom, pouring out all the regret, all the heartache, she'd braved alone.

"Shhh, darlin', shhh." Grams swayed to and fro. It was the same as when she was small and skinned her knees hiking the gravel lane from school—a simple caress, a kind word, and the pain eased.

"Too many people spend their lives lookin' backward, Blair. Ain't nothing to see behind them except the miles already traveled. Worst of all is that you can lose your footin', stumble, and fall. No progress was ever made that way." Grams smoothed the sides of her hair, then cradled her wet cheeks as she spoke her mind. "Matt's retracin' heavy footsteps, relivin' a pain he don't truly understand. A man's gotta know his own heart afore he can offer it to another. Be patient, 'n' believe that anythin' worth havin' don't come easy."

Blair sniffed a fainthearted response. The words were plain and wise, but her needs were complex and great.

Grams sensed her inner conflict. She pursed her lips, held her granddaughter out at arm's length, and spoke in a sigh. "I'm gonna tell you a story I ain't never tole you afore. Sit down, child."

Impressed by her grandmother's strange mood, Blair did her bidding without question. Grams sank into the wicker rocker with a weariness that went beyond her physical state. She began a lazy rock, her voice matching the droning rhythm.

"Your Pa, my son Zachary, was more child of these hills than any of my others. He loved the simplicity, the peace. So, when the time came for him to do his duty and serve his country, he went grudgin'ly. After a spell in Korea he stayed over in St. Louis. That town was like nothin' he'd ever seen before. He was young, easy impressed, and lonely. It was there that he met your mama. She was as lovely as you, and your daddy fell head over heels in love with her."

"I don't understand," Blair interrupted. "I thought—"

"Hush 'n' you will," the matriarch ordered. "They married quickly. Why your ma agreed to wed my Zachary, I'll ne'er know. For she ne'er understood him, of this I'm certain. She thought she could mold him into somethin' he wasn't, but there was too much hill country in him for that. In a year's time they had you and wedded troubles aplenty. Your pa tried to force her to come back to the hills with him, but she loved the bright lights 'n' good times. Finally, when things got too miserable to bear, she told him to go 'n' to take you with him. A babe just didn't fit into her future. I remember the day he come moseyin' up that yonder lane, totin' you, not more than a bundle in his arms. He carried more than just the heartbreak of her runnin' off on him. he was a man who'd lost his will 'n' way. It tweren't that he was weak, mind you. He just left most of his spirit with her."

Grams stared at her long and hard, the motion of the

151

rocker dwindling. "My, but you do favor her," she sighed. "Maybe Zachary mistook the physical likeness for one of the soul? He worried constantly that you'd grow discontented, 'n' one day forsake him like your ma done. He 'n' I had many a discussion over the rebel way of you. I'd argue that it tweren't so much dissatisfaction as strong pride 'n' a hankerin' for somethin' better. He fretted that you were wild 'n' foolish. I can't truly say he was a poor daddy, but he might've been a blind one. Only God knows for sure, I reckon. Been dead nigh on six years now 'n', to tell you the truth, I ain't real sure in my heart that he ever drew another happy breath after leaving your ma."

"Grams, why did you and Pa let me believe my mother died shortly after I was born? If only you'd have told me I had a mother living in St. Louis, I'd have searched for her." Blair couldn't accept the words she'd just heard. It contradicted all she'd believed throughout her life.

"'Cause she did die afore you were three—a car wreck near the train station. Your pa always fooled himself that she was tryin' to make her way back to him, but it tweren't true. After all those years with not a postcard or call, no one will ever convince me that she had a sudden change of heart. I didn't relate this tale to raise your hopes about a ma who turned her back on you. I told you thinkin' it might sustain you in the days ahead." Grams's brittle bones creaked more than the rocker as she forced her body upright from the chair. With a firm hand she beckoned Blair to stand in front of her.

"You got a son to rear, a business to run, a life that won't stand still. You ne'er found peace in these hills cause the turmoil's within you. Yet the spirit's there all the same. Mine and Zachary's blood flows in your veins. You

152

may look like your ma, but you're a one-love person same as your Pa. Preachin' patience is easy enough t' do, practicin' it is another matter. The first time you left, I grieved; this time, I'm tellin' you to go. Return to Dallas, breathe fresh air, and wait on the change of seasons." Her hands clamped tighter, as if the advice she had given was at odds with the dictates of her heart.

"But Danny. He's so happy here. More contented than I've ever seen him. I can't—"

"Nonsense," Grams blurted out. "You can! Danny stays with me. I practically whelped you alone. I figure I can manage. Besides, Matt'll be near. He 'n' the boy ere good for each other. You'll do as I say?" Grams tilted her head, her dark eyes suppressing any objections. Reluctantly Blair nodded.

"Then it's settled." Grams patted her cheek, cleared her throat, and quickly turned from the cherished granddaughter she'd miss terribly. "Supper's in ten minutes. Wash your hands, 'n' don't delay." After the screen door banged shut the only sound was the crisp rustle of September leaves. Like tinkling wind chimes on a breeze, their lonely sound foretold of an oncoming barren season. Her pa had wiled away his life lamenting a fleeting happiness. Why should she believe that fate would be kinder to her?

"Night, Matt," Danny said as Matthew turned out the light and eased toward the door.

He drew up, turning to cast the boy a loving look. "Sleep tight, Danny," he returned, smiling to himself as the boy snuggled deeper beneath the covers and closed his sleepy eyes. Quietly he slipped out the door and headed for the library.

As was his recent custom, he poured himself an ample snifter of brandy, then collapsed into his favorite leather lounger. During his week of guardianship, his days were filled with boyish laughter and long-forgotten energy. Yet, his nights . . . after Danny was tucked in tight and the house echoed with stillness . . . his nights lasted forever. Matt gulped the liquor and stared into space. It was the damnable darkness, alone with his memories and increasing regret, that he dreaded. It was hard enough to cope with the constant reminder of Blair each time he fluffed the boy's copper curls or noted the golden spark in his eyes. But then, at night, as he sat solitary and miserable, her spirit revisited him and his pain ebbed. Her face was everywhere—in the darkened windowpanes, the bottom of his glass; the sound of her voice followed him, even into his empty bed and fitful dreams.

Matt rose and grabbed the bottle from the desk. He slumped back into the chair, poured one more, and drank needily. Was his love never to know an end? Would he ever be free of Blair Logan? In truth, did he really want to be? The questions swirled like the amber liquid in the glass. *Obsessed!* his mind screamed. *Possessed,* his heart concurred. He'd adored her from childhood, and he'd love her until the last breath he drew. She was his beginning, his end—his curse, his prayer.

He refilled his glass once more, as if he preferred oblivion to remembrance. As, in fact, he did. Though Danny had become an integral part of his life—so much so, that he couldn't imagine a day without him—his nights were full of torment, anger, and despair. He ached for Blair, and hated himself for it. He wished for the impossible, and then reviled his weakness. He even found himself damning

154

his dead brother's memory. For it seemed that even from his grave Luke claimed a first and firm right on all that Matt treasured—Blair and Danny. Slowly and surely the latent jealousy eroded a little more of him each passing day. Matt couldn't deal with the guilt—the unforgivable thought that if Luke had never existed, things might have been different. . . . Blair *might have been* his . . . Danny *could have been.* . . .

Matt gulped the smooth, numbing brandy. God! What was he thinking? He loved Luke! They'd shared everything—from baseball cards and a case of the measles to the family car on Saturday night and Sunday morning tales of backseat near-successes. Everything! Including their fatal love for a remarkable woman.

Matt rolled the cool snifter against his cheek. The sedative was beginning to take effect now. Soon he'd think but not feel, remember and not grieve. One more glass and he would stumble down the hall to collapse into his celibate bed; one more glass would obscure the night and hasten the dawn. He poured a last time, downed the merciful contents, then struggled to his feet and left the empty bottle to the quiet room. He made his way up the stairs and down the long hall, then entered the bedroom sanctuary where he and Blair had held off reality for a few precious nights. He tumbled upon the bed, clothes and all, his mind reeling with brandy and reminiscent magic. Oh, God, why did her memory have to be so vivid, the nights so long?

155

CHAPTER ELEVEN

The morning of the day of Blair's return, Danny was bubbling with excitement. Though he loved the time spent with Matt, he adored and missed his mother. As Matt half-listened to his childish babble through breakfast, he fought a sinking sensation. He tried to attribute his anxiety to losing Danny's full-time company. Yet there was something more—an uneasy feeling in the wind. He'd experienced the same kind of premonition once before— the day an Army chaplain had appeared at their front door to tell them of Luke's death. He pretended to concentrate on Danny's homecoming plans for his mother, but his attention drifted. Something—he had no idea what— but something was very wrong.

The front doorbell chimed, and Matt's blue eyes crystallized. Even before rising to answer, he knew a messenger of evil tidings stood on his threshold. Danny started to bolt from his chair, but Matt's firm hand restrained him.

"Finish your breakfast, and then give Navajo his. I'll meet you out back shortly."

"O-kee-doke!" The seriousness of Matt's blue eyes escaped the child as he sopped up maple syrup with a wedge of pancake and then shoved it into his mouth. As Matt passed he couldn't resist ruffling the boy's hair.

He hesitated a moment, peered out the sheer panels,

then opened the door to greet his caller. "Hello, Lloyd. You're up and about early."

Lloyd Prentiss removed his hat as he stepped into the foyer. "Sorry to disturb you afore breakfast, Matt, but it's important."

Matt glanced back to Danny, who was still devouring the stack of hot cakes. "We can talk in the library. Go on in and I'll get us some coffee."

Lloyd shuffled down the hall, then disappeared through the oak doors. Matt retrieved the coffee urn and two cups, giving Danny further instructions on Navajo's grain ration before joining him. He placed the urn and cups on the desk, then eased the library doors shut.

"All right, Lloyd, what is it? You wouldn't be paying me a social call with the chickens unless something's wrong." He poured a cup of coffee and passed it over.

"Thanks," Lloyd muttered, taking a swig, then clearing his throat. "Look, Matt, I think you know I ain't no alarmist. I ain't stupid neither. I'm aware there's no love lost between you and Blair Lo— I mean, Hayden." He squirmed uneasily in his chair, his eyes focusing on the portrait of Luke on the wall.

Matt pretended not to notice, idling over his coffee cup. "Yes?" he prodded.

"Well, even so, I've always believed you a fair man, and probably the only one who can stop what's goin' on."

"I can't if you don't tell me what it is that's exactly going on." Matt's anxiety had begun to show.

"It's that skunk Mason Hershell. He's been out to settle a score with Blair ever since . . ." Lloyd reddened, took another gulp of coffee, then peered up into Matt's unreadable face. "Can we be honest here, Matt?"

157

"Sure," Matt drawled.

"Well, he's been carryin' a grudge ever since she embarrassed him over the Farrett Mine note. It's kinda common knowledge around town," he added.

"Everything usually is." Matt veiled his flaring anger.

"Anyways, Hershell's been spreadin' some mighty scary rumors—sayin' how Hayden Petroleum now runs Farrett Mines, and that the big oil company is gonna replace the local workers with cheap alien labor. He's tellin' everyone who'll listen that their jobs are gonna be gone soon, preachin' layoffs, cutbacks, and hard times." Lloyd rattled off specific instances he'd overheard, then finished off his coffee and slammed it to the desk. "I tell ya, Matt. panic's sweepin' this town like wildfire. It's outa control. The townfolk are in a ugly mood, and all the meanness is directed toward Blair."

Matt was dumbfounded that in his week's absence from his office this disaster could've happened. In his shock he had forgotten his explicit instructions not to be disturbed under any circumstances. He maintained a vigilant silence as Lloyd continued.

"Like I said, Matt, I know you don't owe Blair any favors, but this is hogwash. She's bein' railroaded by that slime Hershell. I watched this town come down on her pretty hard before, and this time I'm bound and determined not to tuck my tail between my legs and do nothin'. I owe her that much."

"Why?"

"What?" Lloyd cocked his head quizzically.

"Why do you feel you owe her?"

"Cause I don't hold with hurtin' someone who ain't never done me any harm. Blair's a good person inside.

158

When we were younger, it didn't seem so bad not to speak up, even when you knew what was bein' said was lies. Now it's different, and the damage we do unto one another ain't kid stuff anymore. I ain't exaggeratin' about the town-folks' mood, Matt. An emergency town meetin' is planned for this evenin'. To tell ya the truth, I'm scared for her and the boy. This could turn out to be a witch hunt. When people are as fired up as these, someone's gonna get burned."

"You think it's that bad?" Matt's grip on the coffee cup tightened.

"I think it's worse." Lloyd stood, nervously fingering the brim of his hat. "Since it's your mine and, in some ways, your town, I just thought you oughta know."

"I appreciate your coming by, Lloyd." Matt extended his hand.

Lloyd hesitated, uncertain if the gesture only meant dismissal or a positive offer of help. "I know there's bad blood between you and her, Matt, but she deserves better than this." He grasped Matt's hand, hoping his words had swayed Farrett's decision.

"I'll see you to the door" was all he received by way of confirmation.

"Naw, that's okay. I can find my way out. Good day to ya, Matt." Lloyd Prentiss stomped from the library and out the front door, feeling scarcely reassured and slightly embarrassed about his visit.

No sooner had Lloyd disappeared from sight than Matt sprung into action. After first phoning the mines to confirm Prentiss's story and then venting his anger at not being apprised of the volatile situation, he hurried to join Danny. He wanted to maintain a mood of normality for the boy. All through the morning he responded to Danny's needs while plotting his campaign.

Later, after giving the boy permission to accompany cook into town, he gathered all the necessary data to disprove Hershell's lies. Once he had organized his plan of attack, he arranged for Danny to stay overnight without prematurely alarming Grams, then retired to the study to await the hour of the town meeting.

Left alone and pensive, Matt felt the minutes tick by slowly. *I know there's bad blood between you and her.* Prentiss's words rang in his head as he sat staring at Luke's portrait. Maybe that was so, but it was a private affair, his inner self argued. He couldn't, wouldn't, stand by and allow evil-minded bigots to malign her. He hadn't forgiven her, but neither would he forsake her.

As his eyes lingered on the painting of Luke, his brother's observation about the town's attitude toward Blair reverberated throughout the quiet room. *I wonder why everyone's so dead set on not giving her a chance. It don't hardly seem fair that just because she hails from the Hollow, people go out of their way to find the bad in her.*

Suddenly Matt yearned for his brother's comradeship. Luke wouldn't falter or fail. He'd always been so strong, so sure. In that lonely instant Matt's eyes rested upon the wooden chest that for years had held Luke's journal upon a shelf. It was the journal he'd kept while in Nam, forwarded along with his other personal effects. Many times before Matt had attempted to read it, but always he closed the pages, unable to stand the pain. But somehow at this particular moment the time seemed right to reach out to his brother.

Slowly Matt rose and walked to the bookcase. Almost

hypnotically he reached for the chest and carried it back to his lounger. Golden sunlight was streaming through the window as he lifted the journal from its lair, opened the pages, and began to read. And as the late-afternoon shadows stretched across the room and he read entry after entry, Matt Farrett discovered a brother, a woman, and a child, he'd never before known. His vision blurred as he read the final entries.

December, '71—Somewhere on the Mekong Delta.

It's damp as hell from what they call the monsoons over here. I've waded in mud until I feel like a damn crawdad. I'm weary tonight. Got a bad case of dysentery too. Every now and then we can hear sniper fire, but after so long it kinda blends with the snores. I've lost track of time. It seems like we been chasin' gooks forever. I wonder how close it is to Christmas.

Christmas! I guess I miss the holidays most. The damn mail is always late. I probably won't get the family's package until Chinese New Year.

Christmas isn't the only thing I wonder about. Most the time I wonder why in the hell I'm here. But then, every so often, I begin to think I understand. That's when I really get scared. Cause when all of this starts making sense, you're ready for a Section Eight. These jungles do things to a man's mind—make him ask questions that, back in the world, might never be considered. Like who you really are, what do you want, and where are you going?

One of them got answered for me today. We're moving on another village tomorrow. There's always one more village, the damn rain, and plenty of V.C.

I saw my first regular about two weeks ago. Stumbled up on him, all alone and cooking something over a makeshift spit. A rat! A goddamn rat!

Must think of something else. The other questions. Who am I really? I don't know for sure. Once I thought I knew everything, but, here, now . . . I don't know. Yeah, I knew all the answers back in Farrett's Corner. I even bluffed Matt into believing I believed it. I let him think I had my life charted for something bigger than running a small-town mine. I thought I did. I knew I hated everything Farrett's Corner stood for. Now I'm not so certain at all. It sure looks good from here. I also know that I'm not the man I was then. I'd handle some things differently. God! I really botched up.

Like Blair. I guess I always knew she loved Matt more than anything else in the world. I wouldn't let her say it though. I needed her—her spirit, her laughter. She brightened my dull life—gave me an inkling of what might exist beyond the hills. All those times we met and talked, it was like glimpsing a future I longed for—excitement, a special woman, love. But really it was Matt's future I saw. Matt's life I botched up. I'm talking in circles. I'm tired and the cramps are worse. Later.

Matt set aside the journal, leaned back in his chair, and closed his eyes. What did Luke's ramblings mean? How weary and discouraged he sounded. A lump formed in Matt's throat, but he reopened the journal and read on.

Christmas Eve '71 Somewhere East of the River.

Found out the exact date a few days ago. Must keep better track of these things. They're important. We took the village and three prisoners. They say they're not V.C., but Intelligence took them for interrogation anyway. I don't know who's the enemy anymore. It's hard to tell. Enemy! That's a strange word. Most the time we fight a ghost we can't see and, when we finally do, every last one of us wishes we never had. It's really not so different than fighting the demons inside yourself. Man! I'm beginning to sound like the bleeding heart Matt said I was. I miss him. I'm sorry for my silence. I know he wonders why I seldom write. I can't.

It's that demon inside. The one who tells me I'm selfish and disloyal. I always knew Blair loved him, but that night when she admitted it, I wished it was me. I guess I hoped that after all was said and done I might take his place. But I was wrong. I couldn't and shouldn't. Because I realize now that I loved the idea of Blair more than anything else. She was daring. Exactly the kind of woman I wanted. Blair gave me an ideal to shoot for. But she wasn't the one for me. I know that now. If only I had then.

I wonder about her often—where and how she is. I think of writing Matt and telling him the truth about his child. I wonder and think, but my guilt eats me alive. I'm afraid he'd hate me for keeping her secret. At the time she seemed so certain that Matt wouldn't understand. And I never gave him a chance to prove otherwise. Instead I offered myself in his place. How selfishly generous I was.

How can I tell him now? What should I say? "Your brother betrayed you"?

You coward! Write him tomorrow. Tell him he has a woman who needs him and child he must be a father to. Tell him how homesick you are for the sight of him. Tell him you were wrong, but, then, weren't we all? He'll forgive you. For Christ's sake, he's your brother! Tomorrow. Do it first chance tomorrow. Maybe tonight you'll sleep without guilt. Won't that feel good. Yeah, it feels better already. I wonder if I have a niece or a nephew? I must tell Matt to write me as soon as he knows. We'll be moving again tomorrow, but I can write when we reach the river. I'm going to give Matt the best Christmas present ever. Later.

There were no more entries, only blank, mud-splattered pages. Luke died on Christmas Day, 1971.

Matt closed the journal, cradled his head between his hands, and cried. So many years later, and almost too late, his brother's Christmas present had been delivered. *Maybe one day we can forgive each other our pride.* Blair's last words to him filled every inch of space in the room. "Forgive me," he moaned to no one. "As I forgive Luke."

CHAPTER TWELVE

An hour before the town meeting Blair's plane touched down at Springfield Airport. As she disembarked she spied Jim Akins standing at the field gates. She adjusted her shoulder-strap flight bag and returned his wave. His presence didn't come as a surprise. Grams had called the night before to tell her that he insisted on picking her up.

As Jim watched Blair's approach he was relieved to see the drawn look she'd departed Farrett's Corner with had been replaced by healthy vitality. Her smile was relaxed, her eyes sparkled, and there was a energetic spring to her stride. Dressed pertly in a tailored three-piece suit, she appeared every inch the executive. She looked absolutely wonderful—as impressive as always. His arm instinctively wrapped around her shoulders as she cleared the gate.

"Dallas agrees with you," he complimented.

"I'm not so sure. Most likely it's only the natural flush of being involved once more. How are you, Jim?" She smiled—the same slow, easy smile he'd missed so very much.

"Except for missing you, I'm fine," he said glibly, guiding her through the maze of parked cars to his station wagon. In a matter of minutes they were cruising the two-lane highway ascending into the hills.

"And how are things in Farrett's Corner?" Blair had no idea that her casual question had struck a nerve. Jim

Akins had also heard the rumors, and was extremely concerned about the explosive mood prevalent in the town. He'd hoped to avoid the subject until the last possible moment. Actually he had more private matters on his mind.

Blair noticed his silent pause. When she glanced at his solemn face, she was immediately put on guard. "Jim? Is anything wrong?"

His grip on the wheel tensed. "Well, I guess that would depend on whose talk you happen to be listening to."

"You're giving me riddles, Jim. From your tone I assume this has something to do with me. Am I supposed to guess who it is that's stirring up trouble for me this time?"

"Mason Hershell," he replied flatly.

"And just what exactly is Mason saying?"

Jim swallowed hard while easing the wagon around a steep curve. "That your big oil conglomerate gobbled up Farrett Mines, and because you have a personal vendetta against the town, soon everyone one will be on welfare or, worse yet, standing in soup lines." There, he'd said it. He didn't dare look her direction.

"Absurd!" she scoffed, her cat's eyes narrowing as she drew erect in the seat.

"Agreed. But nonetheless people are believing it. When virtually a whole town depends on one source of income, they tend to panic when it's rumored to be in jeopardy."

Crimson anger flushed her cheeks. She knew only too well the effects of such unfounded gossip. "I ought to have crushed that sorry excuse of a man when I had the chance."

"Vengeance is mine, saith the Lord." Jim accelerated as they climbed another hill.

166

"Easy for him to say." The sarcastic remark tumbled from her lips before she could check herself. Her tone grew softer with her next words. "I've learned the hard way, Jim, that it's far more effective to turn your back, rather than your cheek, in this town. Why hasn't Matt set things straight?"

"I doubt he knows. Mason Hershell may be a fool, but he's not crazy. Listen, Blair, I'm really concerned for your and Danny's welfare. They're holding a town meeting this evening to air their grievances. I wish you'd make arrangements for both of you to be someplace other than the farm tonight."

"Good grief, Jim! You make it all sound so melodramatic. What do you think they might do? Form a vigilante committee and come lynch me up?"

"And you're taking this much too casually. Yes, I think in the mood these people are in something serious could happen. Don't you understand that you're the target of their frustration?"

The apprehension in Jim's voice stunned her. This was ridiculous! What more satisfaction did these people want from her? Hadn't they persecuted her enough? Would only her complete submission appease them? Blair's chin set stubbornly. She hadn't ever given in before, and she'd be damned if she'd do so now. Especially when she was innocent of any wrongdoing. She felt Jim's gentle clasp of her hand resting on the seat between them.

"I didn't want to be the bearer of bad news on your homecoming, Blair. I hate this senseless anger. If it was within my power to dissuade them, I would. But my words go unheeded, except for Sunday services. I've tried not to look upon it as my failure, but—"

"But nothing," she asserted. "You're a good pastor, Jim Akins . . . a good man. You can't carry Farrett's Corner's sins upon your shoulders. The load would be more than Samson could bear."

He squeezed her fingertips gratefully. "We're coming up on Lake Taneycomo. Would you be opposed to stopping and stretching a bit before traveling on? There's something I wish to say to you before we enter Gomorrah."

She smiled at his innuendo. "Of course not. A breath of fresh air is exactly what I need at the moment."

Jim swung the car onto the road circling the lake. Through the maze of autumn leaves Blair could see the late-afternoon sun sparkling upon the serene waters. The paddleboats and canoes lay deserted and chained to shore, and a tribe of downy little mallards slicked across the glasslike surface behind their proud mother. The tranquility of the scene almost made Blair forget the dilemma which awaited her a few miles ahead. The station wagon rolled to a stop, and they got out of the car.

"Let's walk." Jim took her hand in his, beginning a leisurely stroll along the shoreline. They walked in silence for a while, each wrestling with his inner thoughts.

At last Jim spoke. "Blair?"

"Mmmm," she murmured, staring up at a scarlet cardinal coming to rest on a nearby evergreen.

"This may not be the time to say this, but I've got to speak my mind. Please, Blair, don't say a word until you've heard me out."

She nodded, hoping in her heart she was wrong in her assumption.

"I'm a simple man, Blair—no frills, no mystery. So, I'll

168

state my case plainly. You're a beautiful, intelligent, and loving woman. One that any man would be proud to make his wife. I can't offer you the kind of life you're accustomed to. What I can give you is all my love for the rest of our days. I know it's the wrong season but in your absence my love for you has taken root and blossomed. It's as constant and bountiful as these hills." He drew up, his large, strong hands caressing her fragile shoulders. "I guess what I'm trying to say in my trite and inarticulate way is that I love you, Blair Hayden. And I'd be honored if you'd agree to become this country parson's wife."

Blair lowered her head, unable to meet the hopeful expectancy in his blue eyes. Why? Dear God, why must she hurt this kind and special man? At least Jim deserved to know the truth. Only then might he understand her rejection of his generous offer.

"Unlike you, Jim, I'm not a simple person. I don't mean in a materialistic sense; I mean in my heart." Her voice quavered as she responded. "I wish I could accept to become the wife of such a dear and extraordinary man as you. But, in all honesty, I can't." She felt his grip slacken upon her shoulders. She brushed his cheek with a fingertip and gazed into his soulful eyes.

"I can't because I'm already committed . . . not legally, but in as lasting a bond as any marriage vow. I gave my heart long ago, and have truly only loved one man in my life—Matthew Farrett." She noted the subtle play of emotion that flickered across his face. "I'll tell you something that even Matt doesn't know—Danny is his son. We were so very young, Jim. He was unsure of himself, and I was too proud to influence his decision. Our lives have been a series of misunderstandings, mistrust, and pain. We sac-

169

rificed some of our best years and found no lasting joy. We hurt others and ourselves, and still continue to wound innocent people in our misery. It's got to end. I will not, cannot, make another mistake in the name of pride."

Jim's arm cradled her shoulders as he, once more, set the pace of their walk. He knew she was on the verge of losing all self-control and wished to spare her the embarrassment.

"Surely if you went to Matthew and explained," he suggested.

"No!" she blurted. "The time for confessions have long since passed. Contrary to idealistic belief, confession isn't always good for the soul." She braved a smile, but failed miserably.

"Then what future do the two of you have?"

"None."

"But it's senseless if you love each other," the reverend argued. "In this world, Blair, the chances at real happiness are so few. Why would you choose to disregard the hope, however small, of overcoming the sadness in your lives?"

"Once I would have agreed with you. I would've risked everything for Matt. But, now, after so many disappointments and so much time I've begun to realize that some loves are destructive. I'll always care for him, but I'll never again pursue a love affair which was damned from the start. Each and every time it's brought us, and those we touch, only more pain. Love doesn't necessary conquer all."

She stopped and looked distractedly out over the water. "When we kindled the flame, neither of us had any idea of what it would become. That it would be a ravaging blaze—charring, consuming, stripping barren everything

170

in its destructive path until nothing fertile remained anymore."

"You sound bitter, Blair. You mustn't let this shape your future." Jim gazed long and anxiously at her.

"Not bitter, my dear friend. Resigned," she sighed, her sad eyes slowly shifting from the water back to his distraught face.

"I am your friend, Blair. I will always be. But though I'm disappointed, I refuse to be resigned. I still believe in love, and one day I'll find the perfect woman to share it with."

"And no one will be happier for you than I." She hoped with all her heart his prediction would come true. Rising up on tiptoe, she gently kissed his cheek, thinking how precious the moment when one may truly cherish a friend.

V.F.W. Post 111 was filled to capacity as Arley Simmons struck the gavel to call the town meeting to order. For the past five years Arley always presided over such affairs. No one exactly knew why, but not a soul ever questioned it. As usual Marybeth sat in the front row, as befitted her unofficial first-lady status. She nodded for her husband to begin.

"Oyez, oyez," he boomed, imitating a New England selectman. "The town meetin' is now commencin'."

A shuffle of chairs and coughs went up as the townspeople took their seats, acknowledged their neighbors, and then awaited Arley's next words.

"The reason for this here meetin' is the considerable concern circulatin' throughout our town over recent rumors of layoffs at the mines. From reliable sources it's been said that the mines ain't locally controlled no more.

171

There's good cause to believe a Texas oil firm has bought them out, lock, stock, and barrel, 'n' that hard times lie ahead for us all."

"You don't have to hem-haw around, Arley. All of us know who you're referrin to!" a gruff voice from the back shouted out. People nodded and a few indistinguishable curses went up.

Arley banged the gavel once more. "I was gettin' to that. Simmer down. Well, like the man says, we all know who's behind this trouble. The questions we're debatin' is what's gonna happen now and what do we intend on doin' about it."

"I tell ya what's gonna happen!" A burly fella sitting beside the proper Mason Hershell stood up.

"Speak your peace, Noah."

"Everyone here knows the Hayden woman's got an ax to grind." The crowd murmured in assent. "She justa soon see this town fold as not. She don't care if we got kids to feed and bills to make. Ya think she's gonna cut into her fat profits to oblige us? Hell, no!" Fired by his outspokenness, others began to echo his anger. "We're gonna be weeded out, one by one, till finally this whole town runs dry. And it ain't just us miners who'll suffer—every man, woman, and child will feel the crunch. People'll start movin' elsewhere, whole families will have to begin agin. But the Hollow witch, she won't care. She'll have jest what she's always wanted—our misery."

A few other men came to their feet, waving their doubled fists and yelling seconds.

"She ne'er did give a hoot for none of us. She's bad through and through!"

"Shoulda run her outa town the first time she set foot

172

back here! And it ain't too late yet. We'll show Miss High and Mighty."

"Yeah, well, what about Matthew Farrett? He sold us out too, didn't he? How come he didn't warn us what she was plottin'? Maybe he's in cahoots 'n' gettin' more than jest a fair price?"

"I'll be glad to rebut those accusations. If I may?" All eyes turned to the rear doors and the formidable figure of Matthew Farrett. An instant hush fell over the room.

The dumbfounded Arley Simmons looked to his wife for a sign as to how to proceed. She cocked her head meaningfully toward the rear, telling him to acknowledge Farrett pronto.

"Glad you could make it, Matt." Arley grinned uneasily. "We was jest discussin'—"

"I heard." Matt's commanding voice reverberated throughout the room.

"Well, ah, if ya got somethin' to add, we'd be interested in hearin'," Arley stammered.

"I've got a great deal to say." Matt's wide spread stance told the gathering he meant to stay. "First I find it odd that I was not informed of the nature of this forum. Since *I* am the owner of Farrett Mines and it is to me that most of you look to for your weekly salary, I feel I have a vested interest."

"Well, ah, Matt, since the takeover we jest thought . . ."

"There's been *no* takeover, Arley. Farrett Mines is and always will be mine."

A surprised rumble filtered through the room. Eyes turned toward Mason Hershell, who sat cool and collected, staring dead ahead.

"I have in my possession papers which will substantiate that fact for those of you who feel inclined to question my word. I must tell you, though, that I'd consider it an insult when you so easily accept the word of an *outsider*. I'd advise instead that you spend the time checking your accounts at Farrett Mercantile."

Hershell leapt to his feet. "What are you implying?"

Matt's eyes glinted dangerously. "What are you guilty of, Mason?"

The tension in the room became almost tangible until an anxious voice from up front broke up the face-off between the two men. "So, what ere ya sayin', Matthew? That our jobs ere secure?" Slowly Mason resumed his seat.

"Your jobs are secure," Matt answered, his eyes and stance becoming less threatening.

"Well, I'll be damned. You mean all this hoopla was for nothin'?" Arley expressed the general sentiment of the crowd.

"Maybe not," Matt suggested. "Maybe there's a lesson to be learned. This town's always been fast to jump to conclusions and much too quick to judge. I know. I've been as guilty as the rest of you. You scoff at what you don't understand and mock what you can't control—such as someone like Blair Hayden."

Rachel Prentiss sprung up from her chair. "I'm not believin' my ears! You, of all people, are fixin' to lecture us about Blair Logan?" Her indignant voice became nearly a screech.

"Yes, Rachel. I don't think anyone better than I has the right."

"Well, ain't you the pious one!" Rachel jerked her arm free from her husband's silent demand to sit back down.

174

"No, not pious. I think *embarrassed* might be a better word. You see, Rachel, I've recently discovered that I've been a very callous and blind man. I misjudged and mistreated Blair because I only viewed her through the eyes of prejudice. I've been wrong, and so have all of you. She's committed no wrong against any of us. Her only sin is one of silence—a silence born of pride. Once I turned my back on her for what I imagined to be good reason, only to find out that all that I believed about her was wrong. And for that rash and foolish mistake I forfeited ten years with my son."

The ladies gasped, the men lowered their heads, and Rachel Prentiss sank dazedly to her chair.

"I don't say this lightly. I only confirm what is true. I plan to beg Blair's forgiveness and try to make this up to my boy. I only pray it's not too late." Matt spoke as if to himself, his eyes blank and his voice low. Then, seeming to remember himself, his gaze lurched up and he looked out upon the astonished faces. "But, regardless of Blair's answer, I remind you all that I admire her greatly, and that the boy is a Farrett. I beseech your long-overdue acceptance, but I demand your respect for them both."

Without another word or backward look, Matt squared his proud shoulders, then exited the still room.

"Well, can you beat that!" Rachel shook her head disbelievingly.

"No, but I'd give a week's wages to wail the tar outa you!" Lloyd grabbed her arm, jerking her up from the chair and out the side door.

Just before the door slammed to, her whine of "I don't understand, Lloyd. What are ya so mad at me for?" drifted over the pensive gathering.

* * *

Blair and Jim's conversation ceased as they heard the rumble of the Cherokee outside. They looked in the direction of the slam of the jeep door, then exchanged hesitant glances.

"Tell him," Jim urged just as Matt reached the back door.

She shook her head adamantly no, then crossed the room to answer his knock.

"We need to talk, Blair" was all Matt said as he brushed past her into the room. He drew up rigid at the sight of Rev Akins.

"I was just leaving, Matt." Jim diplomatically excused himself, reaching for his jacket and starting for the door.

"Must you?" Blair's voice held a pleading note.

"I'm afraid so." He smiled at her encouragingly, nodded farewell to Matt, then stepped out upon the porch and breathed a sigh of crisp mountain air. As Blair stood watching his easy progress to the car, she felt a terrible emptiness welling up within her. Vaguely she returned his wave, and then turned to face the solemn Matt.

"Would you care for something? Coffee? Tea?"

"Some honest conversation would be nice." His expression was impregnable, not a clue to his intent.

"If you've come to play word games, Matt, I'm warning you that I'm in no mood." Blair put distance between them as she pretended to rearrange the throw pillows on the sofa.

"I understand another monumental town meeting was held tonight. Have you heard yet what our illustrious town fathers have decreed as my penance? Is it to be

176

crucifixion or something simpler, like burning the witch at the stake?" She banged a pillow with a vengeance.

"I attended," he stated flatly.

"Oh?" she replied in a caustic tone. "And how did you cast your vote? Fire or nails?"

"Stop it, Blair!" He took a step forward; she retreated. "The only reason I went at all was to defend you," he quietly explained. "Not only did I set them straight on the mine's status, but on a few other matters as well. I don't think you'll have any more problems."

Foolishly clutching a pillow to her chest as if it could somehow shield her, she stared at him for a meditative moment. "I appreciate your intercession on my behalf, Matt," she finally said. "Of course, had I been allowed to speak in my own defense, your gallant gesture would've been unnecessary." Instinctively Blair felt threatened. Intense undercurrents hovered in the room—almost an air of a fencing match. Defensively she assumed an en garde position.

Matt pressed his aggressor's advantage with a testing nick of her defenses. "I was protecting Danny's interests. After all, he's a Farrett, isn't he? More heir to the Farrett dynasty than the Hayden fortune?"

Blair sensed him closing in, felt her derisory defenses crumbling. His attitude told her he suspected the truth, but long-practiced survival instincts insisted that she rally and fight.

"True," she parried coolly. "But I don't feel that the agreement we've reached threatens Danny's inheritance or needs public championing. I've sheltered him from scavengers before and, I might add, protected his interests without exposing them to public scrutiny. I won't under

177

any circumstances vindicate myself at the cost of exposing Danny's Farrett connection!"

Matt's expressive eyes glinted like crystal prisms, his voice taking on the keen edge of tempered steel as he adroitly deflected her thrust. "Since I never acquired your talent for remaining silent, I'm afraid your demand comes a little too late. I've already openly acknowledged Danny's rightful place in Farrett's Corner."

Staring deep into those azure eyes which at once spoke of torment and implacability, she experienced a dismal sensation of foreboding. Icy tendrils of dread wrapped around her heart. As her body reflexively stiffened and she struggled for a composing breath, a muffled drumbeat resounded in her head.

"How dare you take it upon yourself to interfere in our lives! You have no right! Damn your presumption! And damn you, Matthew Farrett!" An uncontrollable trembling seized her bottom lip. She hurled the pillow at him, betraying the fine edge she was teetering on. Her frayed nerves could not withstand the strain of what she knew to be forthcoming—an unconditional surrender to the truth.

Matt realized her pain, commiserated with her. Yet his only chance of salvaging a future that would fulfill his most fervent hopes was to force that very pain to the surface, and then deal with the repercussions afterward.

"I have no right?" he almost shouted. "Have you been living a lie so long, Blair, that you're beginning to believe it yourself?" He stepped nearer, then winced at the sudden ache her instant withdrawal caused. "Blair . . ." His voice grew hoarse, his speech deliberate. "Why do you persist in denying my right to claim and protect Danny? Is it so hard to admit that he's *my son?*"

178

A low, miserable groan of "Dear God!" escaped her colorless lips as, simultaneously, his distraught face swayed before her and she buckled beneath a descending weight.

In one swift motion Matt swept her up in his brawny arms and held her close against his hammering heart. Her copper hair spilled in disarray around her pallid features as she collapsed weakly against his shoulder, murmuring over and over, "You know . . . you know . . . ."

"Yes, Blair, I know that he's mine, just as you would've been years ago if not for my prideful stupidity." She buried her head deeper into his shoulder, muffling the sobs that racked her slim form. Matt nestled his cheek in her fragrant hair, whispering brokenly, "Curse me, damn me with my own ignorance but, please, Blair, for the sake of all that's sacred between us, don't reject me." He held her tighter, pressing his wet cheek against hers and praying for absolution.

"Oh, Matt," she moaned, lifting her agonized eyes to his pleading ones. "We've put ourselves through so much pain and regret. Do we dare dream that there's an end to it?"

"You dream, tomboy; I'll make it real," he pledged, his tender kiss prefacing a lifetime of devotion before he carried her out the door to the Cherokee.

Whisking her from the Hollow and high up into the mountains, Matt kept his promise. From the moment he carried her over the threshold of Farrett House and up the winding staircase to gently lay her on his poster bed, she became more than just the new mistress of the estate; she became the mistress of his heart.

So long they had waited for this moment, too often

179

giving up hope that it would ever come to pass. Now, as
he had pledged, the dream became real as Matt slowly,
almost reverently, undressed her. He knew he had a lifetime in which to savor her. No longer were they con-
demned to stolen moments, a shadowed love. Tonight,
with a last drop of Matt's clothing to the floor, their love
affair would truly begin—a union as rich and fulfilling as
it was meant to be from the start. For theirs was a special
love—one that had endured past heartbreak and deserved
this present joy.

They caressed one another as if they'd never touched
before, kissed with the passion of virgin lovers, bared and
shared themselves wholly, and then reveled in the reincar-
nation of two lost souls. For, in truth, never in their entire
lives had they been so free, so fresh, so sure.

"I remember our first kiss, Matt." A sigh of nostalgia
escaped her. "My lips were parched from too much sun,
but yours . . ." She smiled wistfully up at him, tracing the
outline of those memorable lips with a fingertip. ". . . yours
were cool like the dippin' spring. I drank and drank of
you, unable to quench my thirst. And after all these years,
I still can't get my fill. Kiss me, Matt. Kiss me long, kiss
me easy."

Instantly, his protective arms enfolded her, drawing her
fast against his muscular length. Tenderly and thoroughly
his moist lips and expert tongue abated her thirst.

"Mmmm, again," came her husky entreaty as her
fingers entwined within his hair, drawing his life-giving
mouth upon hers once more. The feel of those sating lips
was so singular, so divine, that she tremored with the
sheer wonder they evoked. He was a shimmering oasis in
a desert of discontent; a well spring by which to stave off

180

the aridity of this world. He refreshed and replenished her. She drank greedily and needfully from his well of love. And still, she thirsted for more.

Like desert wanderers, her hands roamed his flesh in quenchless delirium. The trail of her arousing touch singed Matt's sensitive skin. He burned with an insatiable need—one which only she could ignite and quell. Yet, the glide of her palms across his back, over his buttocks, and up his hips, the sensuous feel of her supple body beneath his, the soft pressure of her tantalizing mouth, and velvet probe of her tongue induced such sweet agony that he yearned to prolong it. For she was the smell of fragrant jasmine, the feel of sleek satin, the grace of a willow and the caress of a summer breeze.

"Blair." Her name came softly against her swollen lips. "I've loved you for so many long, wasted years." His adoring gaze held hers as he brushed back her tumbled, flame tresses from her beautiful face—the face he'd re-created in dreams and envisioned in waking, empty space. "But there's no place for regret in our lives anymore. There's only this moment and those we'll share hereafter. I loved you then, Blair Logan, but not nearly as much as I love you now." At the sight of welled tears in her topaz eyes, his hand gently cupped her cheek.

"Then, you forgive me for the years I kept Danny from you," she whispered.

He clutched her close, tripping light kisses across her dainty forehead. "To ask forgiveness of each other only wastes more precious time."

"There's one thing I have to know, Matt. Then, I prom-ise the past won't ever come between us again." She felt his arms tighten about her, as if bracing himself for what would follow. She looked up into his blue eyes, easing his apprehension with a smooth stroke against his cheek. "How did you learn the truth about Danny?"

His gaze relaxed as he caught her hand and thoughtfully kissed its palm. "Luke told me," he said with a sigh. At her confused look, he explained. "His journals . . . I finally read them. Little did I realize that of all the things Luke and I ever shared his last words would be the most significant."

They cuddled close and then, wrapped in the warmth of one another, sank deeper within the feather pillow. Outside, a sudden autumn rain sheathed the purple hills. It was a quiet time—a time of soft touches, hushed words, and gentle love; a time of late-harvesting and abundance, full moons and complete joy. And as Matt's lithe body covered hers and they rhythmed their love to the patter of falling rain, serenity melded their hearts as much as passion united their bodies. For with this night and the enactment of love's blessed union came their beginning. No more secrets or heartache could come between them. They were one; inseparably whole.

A week later, on a clear and crisp autumn afternoon when one could see forever, Matt consummated the commitment made over a decade ago.

Most of Farrett's Corner turned out for the festive occasion. After all, this event was considered to be nearly as important as the catfish fry. Beneath the Ozark sun, shining warm and golden, and amid the splendor of the multicolored hills, the striking couple stood upon Farrett land, repeating the vows Jim Akins recited. As the reverend performed the ceremony he spoke with a conviction

182

that echoed the supreme test this love had survived. But though his words rang with unusual strength, his smile held a secret joy.

A starched and beaming Grams sat in the front row. Every now and then her hanky would dab at her bright brown eyes. Periodically she'd glance at another guest on her right or left, raise her chin proudly, and favor him with a polite nod, as if to say, "Fine day for a weddin'."

According to matrimonial protocol, the best man, Daniel Farrett, stood at his father's right. Most grown-up-looking in his new suit and tie, he behaved admirably until the time came to produce the sacred ring. Instead of merely relinquishing it, the boy hesitated. Then, with a grin of sheer delight, he kissed his mother's cheek, hugged his father's broad shoulders, and pressed the gold band into the groom's hand. Matt's blue eyes filled as he clasped his son's shoulder and placed him between Blair and himself. He wanted the boy to be a part of the moment when he slipped the band, inscribed with the one word *Forever* onto his beloved's third finger.

"I now pronounce you man and wife." Jim Akins's melodious voice pealed like resounding church bells. "What God has joined together let no man put asunder. You may kiss the bride."

"This is the good part, Matt," Danny whispered.

"I know, son. Believe me, I know." Matt's smile reflected the peace which now filled his life. His crystal-blue eyes mellowed with love as he slowly drew Blair into his strong arms, then kissed her with a depth and devotion that symbolized the romance they shared. Every guest present could feel the magic. Danny, however, not yet having been privy to such a foreign emotion at last broke the spell,

183

whistling aloud and exclaiming, "Wow, Matt! That's some kinda kiss!" Instantly his parents separated with an embarrassed laugh, Matt hugging Blair close with one arm and ruffling his rascal son's curls with his free hand.

Well-wishers crowded round. The joyful Blair had only time for a quick embrace of her grandmother before assuming her new duties as mistress of Farrett House. As she sliced and served the tiered bridal cake, her hazel eyes glowed each and every time they fell upon her handsome husband. To be his wife was more than just a dream come true; it was destiny fulfilled. For though it had taken many years and immeasurable pain, she now knew Matt's love to be as eternal as these glorious hills. Their winter season would be one of content. When the first fleecy snows capped the mountains and the valley lay dormant beneath fields of white powder, they would cuddle close by a crackling fire and nurture one another with their warmth. Their love would know many seasons; much happiness, passion, and silent pride—a pride that comes from knowing that, no matter what the unforeseen problems, the union would prevail.

As Lloyd and Rachel Prentiss approached to pay their respects, Blair bestowed a benevolent smile upon Rachel. No longer did she harbor any resentment or malice in her heart. For as the wise Grams had once said, "No progress was ever made lookin' backward". Blair Logan Farrett would never again look to the past. Her future was too rich, too full. Finally the rebel would know peace. At last she'd come home.

LOOK FOR NEXT MONTH'S
CANDLELIGHT ECSTASY ROMANCES ®

THE DARK HORSEMAN

Marianne Harvey

author of *The Proud Hunter*

Beautiful Donna Penroze had sworn to her dying father that she would save her sole legacy, the crumbling tin mines and the ancient, desolate estate *Trencobban*. But the mines were failing, and Donna had no one to turn to. No one except the mysterious Nicholas Trevarvas—rich, arrogant, commanding. Donna would do anything but surrender her pride, anything but admit her irresistible longing for *The Dark Horseman*.

A Dell Book $3.50

THE TAMING

Aleen Malcolm

Cameron—daring, impetuous girl/woman who has never known a life beyond the windswept wilds of the Scottish countryside.

Alex Sinclair—high-born and quick-tempered, finds more than passion in the heart of his headstrong ward Cameron.

Torn between her passion for freedom and her long-denied love for Alex, Cameron is thrust into the dazzling social whirl of 18th century Edinburgh and comes to know the fulfillment of deep and dauntless love.   **$3.50**

At your local bookstore or use this handy coupon for ordering:

Desert Hostage

Diane Dunaway

Behind her is England and her first innocent encounter
with love. Before her is a mysterious land of forbidding
majesty. Kidnapped, swept across the deserts of
Araby, Juliette Barclay sees her past vanish in the
endless, shifting sands. Desperate and defiant, she
seeks escape only to find harrowing danger, to
discover her one hope in the arms of her captor, the
Shiek of El Abadan. Fearless and proud, he alone can
tame her. She alone can possess his soul. Between
them lies the secret that will bind her to him forever, a
woman possessed, a slave of love. **$3.95**